PRAISE FOR SHION MIURA'S
THE GREAT PASSAGE

Winner of an Earphones Award, Fiction

"Mastery of words may not result in masterly communication, and a great dictionary, like a love story, is 'the result of people puzzling over their choices'—a classic tension that has made *The Great Passage* a prizewinner in Japan, as well as both a successful feature film and an animated television series."

—*The New York Times*

"Swirling with witty enchantment, *The Great Passage* proves to be, well, utterly great. Readers should be advised to get ready to sigh with delighted satisfaction and awe-inspiring admiration."

—*Booklist* (starred review)

"*The Great Passage* has a philosophy of thoughtfulness and dedication to words that any reader will understand . . . Miura's prose—and Carpenter's translation—glides along, smooth and precise, with flashes of quiet poetry."

—*Metropolis*

"*The Great Passage* is interwoven with romantic love stories, but ultimately it is the passion of the characters, their friendship, and their devotion to their task that direct and complete the narrative and turn it from simply a good book to a great one."

—Talia Franks, Three Percent

THE
EASY LIFE
IN
KAMUSARI

THE EASY LIFE IN KAMUSARI

BOOK 1 IN THE FOREST SERIES

SHION MIURA

TRANSLATED BY JULIET WINTERS CARPENTER

AMAZON **CROSSING**

Japanese names are written given name first, except in the Acknowledgments and Main References sections, where the surname is first and macrons are used to indicate long vowels.

Text copyright © 2012 by Shion Miura
Translation copyright © 2021 by Juliet Winters Carpenter
All rights reserved.

Previously published as 神去なあなあ日常 (Easy Life in Kamusari) by 徳間書店 / Tokuma Shoten in Japan in 2012 in care of Tuttle-Mori Agency, Inc., Tokyo. Translated from Japanese by Juliet Winters Carpenter. First published in English by Amazon Crossing in 2021.

Published by Amazon Crossing, Seattle

www.apub.com

Amazon, the Amazon logo, and Amazon Crossing are trademarks of Amazon.com, Inc., or its affiliates.

ISBN-13: 9781542027151 (hardcover)
ISBN-10: 1542027152 (hardcover)

ISBN-13: 9781542027168 (paperback)
ISBN-10: 1542027160 (paperback)

Cover design by Rex Bonomelli

Printed in the United States of America

First edition

THE
EASY LIFE
IN
KAMUSARI

1

A Guy Named Yoki

Kamusari villagers are really easygoing, especially those living deep in the mountains. They often use the expression *naa-naa*, which might sound negative but means something like "take it easy," "relax." It can even be a greeting. Two villagers passing on the road might have the following exchange:

"Naa-naa." (Lovely day.)

"Mm-hm."

"Your man on the mountain?" (Has your husband left already to work in the forest?)

"Says today he'll be a holler away so he'll naa-naa after lunch. A body can't even vacuum with him around, so I'm in a fix." (He says he's working on a nearby mountain today, so he'll take his time and go over after lunch. I can't get my cleaning done with him in the way, so I'm upset.)

In the beginning, I often had trouble making out what they were saying. Kamusari is in Mie, near the prefectural border with Nara, and the local dialect is similar to the drawl of western Japan. Villagers often tag their sentences with a soft "*na*," which adds on another layer of calm.

"Got over your stomachache, na."

"Yeah."

"Heard you ate too much, na."

"Probably, na."

Laid back as they are, they do get worked up on occasion. I once heard Nao scold a little kid: "I said no first grader plays in the river unless he's with a grown-up! Do it again and I'll give you what for! A *kappa*'ll come and steal your *shirikodama*!" (Kappa, river imps, are supposed to have designs on human shirikodama, the soul-ball located inside the anus.) As for who Nao is, I'll get to that later.

Anyway, threatening a kid with kappa in this day and age? Really? And what's the deal with shirikodama? There's no such thing in *my* butt, that's for sure. But the kid wailed, "No kappa, they're scary! I won't do it anymore, promise! I'm sorry!" He was on the verge of tears. Talk about innocent. It's as if all the villagers stepped out of a folktale.

Soon it'll be a year since I left my hometown of Yokohama and came here to live. I decided to write down everything that's happened in the last twelve months. Life here strikes me as pretty unusual. The people are funny in a way. They seem so mild-mannered, but then they'll quietly say or do something totally destructive.

I wonder if I can make a go of it here. I don't know yet, but anyway I decided to try writing down everything. The dusty computer in Yoki's place turned on when I plugged it in, so that helps, but it's not hooked up to the internet. He uses a black dial phone—first one I ever saw—and none of the rooms in his house has a cable outlet. I wonder why he bought a computer in the first place? Maybe he was just curious. I bet after he bought it, reading the instruction manual was too much trouble so he just let it sit there.

As for who Yoki is, I'll get to that.

I've never written anything very long, but making a written record will probably help me relax, Kamusari-style, and sort out my feelings.

There's not as much work to do in the winter, so I'll have plenty of time to write.

I figure there are a couple of reasons why Kamusari villagers are so easygoing. One is that most of them are involved in forestry, where you have to think in cycles of a century; the other is that there's no place to hang out at night, so when it gets dark everybody just hits the hay. "Running around won't make the trees grow faster. Get plenty of rest, eat hearty, and tomorrow take what comes": that seems to be the prevailing philosophy.

Lately, without really meaning to, I've started ending my sentences with "na," too. But I'm still not up on the local speech enough to reproduce it on paper. Just imagine if you will that everybody's speaking Kamusari dialect all the time. Not that I have the slightest intention of ever showing this to anyone. But it's kind of cool, isn't it? To pretend I have readers and be like, "Bear in mind as you read, everybody's speaking Kamusari dialect"?

Or not.

Anyhow, I'll just go ahead and write down what happened this year, as it comes to mind. Sit back and relax. Whoever you are—*heh heh*.

I always figured that after high school I'd be a "freeter"—a temp worker. My grades weren't great, and I never liked studying, so neither my parents nor my teachers ever advised me to "give college a try." I didn't feel like getting a company job, either: the idea of settling into a lifelong groove at eighteen turned me off.

Right up until graduation day, I worked part-time in a convenience store. Killing time, basically. I knew I couldn't go on like that forever, that without a real job I wouldn't have much of a future, and people around me were telling me that, too. But the idea of a "future" twenty or thirty years down the line didn't really click with me. I tried not to think about it. I didn't have anything in particular I wanted to do, and

I didn't expect I ever would. That's as far as I got. I thought that after graduation, nothing would change, that my life would go right on the same as ever.

But after the ceremony, Kumayan (that's what I call Mr. Kumagai) told me, "Well, Hirano, I found you a job."

Who asked him to do a thing like that? My jaw dropped. "What? You're kidding."

Turns out he wasn't kidding.

Kumayan took me home and lo and behold, Mom had already started moving her stuff into my room. Exercise equipment she'd bought online and never used, stuff like that.

"I sent some clothes and other things you'll need ahead to Kamusari village," she said. "Listen to what they tell you. Do your best. Here, this is from your father."

Kamusari village? Where was that? I was reeling.

She handed me a white envelope from my old man, who was still at work. It was marked "Going-away money." Inside was thirty thousand yen. What was I supposed to do with a measly thirty thousand yen?

"Screw this!" I shouted. "This is tyranny! What's the big idea?"

Mom opened a notebook in her hand and started reading aloud. *"Only the moon never sleeps. From the window, it peers in on my heart."*

Crap, she was reading from *Book of My Poems*! I lunged at her in mute fury. Dammit, I'd kept that hidden in my desk drawer. "Give it back!"

"No. Unless you want me to make copies and share them with your friends, off you go to Kamusari like a good boy."

What a way to treat her sensitive teenage son. She was a mean, cold-blooded witch. Even now, just thinking about it makes me furious. But I never was much for decisive action, even though my name means "courage."

"Well, well," said Kumayan. "'Only the moon,' eh? 'Never sleeps,' eh?" He chuckled. "Don't worry, I won't tell."

I wished the whole human race would drop off the face of the earth.

Anyway, I fell into my mom's trap and had no choice but to leave. My old man's salary had recently taken a hit, so she couldn't wait for me to be off on my own. My brother and his wife lived around the corner, and they'd just had a baby; that was part of it, too. Mom was so wrapped up in her first grandkid, I got shunted aside. My old man is chronically under her thumb. He'd better be careful or he'll be next out the door.

Kumayan took me to Shin Yokohama Station and put me on the bullet train. He pressed a piece of paper into my hand with instructions on how to get to Kamusari.

"You can't come back for a year. Take care of yourself, Hirano. Hang in there."

I eventually found out that, without telling me, they had signed me up for a government-sponsored program called Green Employment. The idea is to support the reemployment of people returning to their hometowns or moving to rural areas for the first time. People fresh out of high school like me are the exception. That they would even consider the application of someone like me shows how shorthanded the forestry industry is. For the first year of training, each participating forestry union and company gets a subsidy of three million yen per trainee. Of course, that has to cover costs for trainees and their trainers, plus material and equipment, so it's peanuts. But in mountainous regions with few young people, villagers are eager to provide training in forestry, happy to think somebody has finally come along who's willing to continue the business. Escape is impossible. Confronted by the three million yen subsidy and the villagers' joy and devotion, no decent human being could choke out the words, "I quit."

I got off the bullet train in Nagoya and changed to the Kintetsu line, going as far as Matsusaka, then swaying and bouncing on a local line I'd never heard of, going deeper and deeper into the mountains. Still clueless about what lay ahead and smarting from my unceremonious eviction, I felt uneasy and frustrated and lonely, but at the same time I figured, *What the heck. Might as well play along and see what happens.* I felt like I was on an adventure, a safari.

On the way, I texted a friend: Out of the blue Kumayan packed me off to some place called Kamusari.

I got a quick reply: For real? Oh wow. Cool.

After a while the signal died. No reception. I couldn't believe it. Was this still Japan? I gave up and looked out the window.

The local train had just one car. Maybe it was a bus that ran on tracks? There was nothing on the roof to collect power and no power lines that I could see. No conductor, either. The driver collected tickets as passengers got off. There were four of us to start with, and pretty soon, besides me, there was only an old lady eating tangerines. At the station before mine, she tottered off.

The local bus or train or whatever it was ran alongside a mountain stream. The farther upstream we went, the clearer the water became. I'd never seen a river so clean. The mountainsides came closer and closer, until finally you couldn't tell they were mountains anymore. It was like riding straight through a forest. The ground, lightly blanketed with snow, was covered with cedars. (Actually some of them were cypresses, but at the time I didn't know one tree from another.)

When it gets warm, the locals must really suffer from hay fever. I was just thinking this as we came to the end of the line. It was a small, unmanned station, and when I got out and stood on the platform, the air was cool and moist. No sign of houses. The silhouettes of the surrounding mountains soon sank into the darkness.

As I stood there outside the old station house, wondering what next, a white pickup truck came zooming down the road, passing other cars on the way, and stopped in front of me. A big fellow got out of the driver's seat and came over. He made me jump a little. With short hair dyed bright yellow, he looked every inch a gangster.

"Yuki Hirano?"

"Yes."

"You got a phone?"

"Right here." I brought it out from my jeans pocket and he snatched it up. "Hey, wait a minute!"

I tried to grab it back, but he was faster. He took out the battery pack and hurled it through the trees. I heard it land in the river with a faint splash.

"What'd you do that for?"

"Take it easy. You won't need a phone here. No reception."

This was criminal. I was appalled, and the grinning stranger gave me the willies, so I turned around and went back into the station house. *That does it. I'm going home.* But there were no more trains for Matsusaka. The last one had left at 7:25. *Give me a break.*

I went back outside. He was still standing there.

"Get in." He tossed me my lightened phone. "Hurry it up. Any luggage?"

All I had was a backpack with a change of clothes. He put it in the bed of his pickup and motioned to me with his chin. He couldn't have been more than thirty. He looked muscular and strong, and he had quick reflexes, too. He was crazy enough to say hello to a person by grabbing their phone battery and throwing it away, so I decided not to resist. In any case, I couldn't make my move till morning. Sleep in a deserted station building way in the mountains and get mauled by wild dogs? No, thanks. I got in the passenger seat.

"I'm Yoki Iida." That's all he said.

He drove the pickup deeper into the mountains, speeding up a narrow, twisting road for about an hour. My ears popped. We had to be climbing pretty high. This Yoki was a wild driver; at every curve in the road, I swayed right or left. I got a little carsick.

My backpack and I were deposited by a building like an assembly hall. Yoki drove off, and an older guy who'd been expecting me served stew for supper.

"It's wild boar." He beamed.

I was legit eating wild boar stew.

After he'd laid out my futon in a small room like a night watchman's quarters, the guy left, leaving me alone in the building. All I could hear was the murmur of the river and the rustle of leaves. The quiet got to me. I pressed my forehead against the windowpane and looked outside, but there was only blackness. No scenery, nothing. It was almost April, but the cold settled in my bones.

Out in the corridor there was a pink telephone, so I called home.

"Oh, Yuki! You made it there okay?" Behind Mom's voice I heard a baby laughing. My brother and his wife must've come over.

"Yeah. I ate wild boar stew."

"That's nice. I've never had it. Was it good?"

"Yeah. Or, I dunno, I mean, what is this place? What am I gonna do here?" *I wanna come home.* Pride made me bite the words back.

"Do? Well, work, of course."

"Work how?"

"It's a miracle there was *any* job for you, so buckle down and do your best. You won't know if it suits you till you've given it a try."

"What kind of job is it? What's the deal?"

"Oh, I think the bath is ready!" With this lame excuse, she hung up.

Great. Some mother. Packed me off here without even bothering to find out what kind of work I'll be doing. I crawled under the covers, leaving the kerosene stove on, so anxious and troubled I could have cried. I might actually have shed tears.

In the morning, I learned I was in the office of the forest owners' cooperative. What was that? Would I be working here? I had a ton of questions. As it turned out, that was the start of three weeks' basic training. Wild Boar Stew Guy gave lectures with titles like "Dangers That Lurk in the Mountains" and "Forestry Terminology." I learned how to use a chain saw. Got yelled at constantly: "Put your back into it! Keep your arm up high!" And so at last, the truth hit me: I'd been sent here to work in forestry.

Forestry? No way. No frigging way! That's what I thought, but during the daytime when the local line was running, the guy stuck to me like glue. Even then, three times I seized an opening and made a dash for it, but each time he caught me and hauled me back to the office. His biceps were huge. Turned out he was famous for his ability to grab a wild boar in the forest and hurl it.

So I had no choice but to settle down and go on with the training. Even so, I stayed on the alert, perpetually on the lookout for another chance to bolt.

"You'll learn a lot working under Nakamura-san," he told me. "Do your best."

Nakamura-san? Who's that? I wondered. He said no more.

When the three weeks of basic training ended, Yoki Iida came back for me in his pickup truck. I got in and was whisked still farther upstream. Wild Boar Stew Guy stood in the doorway and waved till I couldn't see him anymore. I felt like the doomed calf in the song "Donna Donna."

All that chain saw practice had left me with a sore back and blistered palms. Every muscle ached, and I walked bowlegged. The training left no doubt in my mind: I was not cut out to be a mountain man. But the words *Let me go home* wouldn't come. Escape didn't seem possible.

Yoki gripped the steering wheel, moody and uncommunicative.

Kamusari village is divided into three districts. The farmers' cooperative is in the middle one, Naka district. Yoki was taking me to Kamusari district, the remotest part of the village, a thirty-minute drive up the road. Kamusari district is so deep in the mountains, there's hardly any level ground. A hundred or so people live in a scattering of several dozen houses along the Kamusari River. Each family grows its own vegetables in a back garden, and there's a communal rice paddy in a stretch of flat land by the river. Most of the residents are over sixty. A single store sells necessities. There's no school or post office. To buy stamps or mail a package, you ask the mailman when he comes around.

To send a package by home delivery service, you have to go all the way to Naka district. The nearest place to go shopping is a town called Hisai, several mountains away.

In other words, the very picture of inconvenience.

Yoki drove across a narrow bridge and parked in front of someone's house. "Let's go say hello to the master."

The *master*? As I was registering this word from another era, Yoki started walking up a gentle slope, never looking back. I hurried after him. A wintry wind blew down from the mountain. Snow lay in crannies along the path. We didn't encounter anyone else along the way. Not that I expected to see many people in the boondocks—and besides, it was lunchtime.

The master's house was planted on an elevation slightly removed from the river, with its back to a low mountain. It was an old, solid, traditional farmhouse that seemed literally planted where it stood. The spacious front yard was spread with evenly sized white gravel. In one corner was a wood-plank table and benches. The table was enormous, big enough to seat a crowd at a barbecue. By the front door, I saw two outsize nameplates. One read "Nakamura" and the other, "Nakamura Lumber Co."

So Nakamura-san was the master. And this, apparently, was where I'd be working. What could the master look like? Full of curiosity, I followed close behind Yoki. Not bothering to ring the doorbell, he opened the door, and from the dim interior a little boy about five years old came running. Big, round eyes, light skin, red cheeks.

"Yoki!" he yelled in delight, arms wide open.

"Hey there, Santa." Yoki scooped him up. "Your daddy here?"

"Yeah!"

As I eventually found out, "Santa" is written with characters meaning "mountain man"; no connection to reindeer and elves.

Carrying the boy, Yoki entered the house, heading down a dim passageway to a big kitchen with an earthen floor. I looked around curiously, having never seen an old-fashioned kitchen before. The open beams were black with soot. A section of the ceiling was boarded off to create storage space; a wooden ladder led up to it.

Santa watched me with great interest, peering over Yoki's shoulder as I took it all in. When our eyes met, he shyly ducked down and put his forehead against Yoki's shoulder. Soon he raised his head timidly and looked at me again. This time when our eyes met, he smiled. Cute little bugger.

Probably to keep out the cold, the door to the rest of the house was shut. It had a black sheen. Yoki pushed it open with one hand and stuck his head inside.

"Hey, Seiichi. The new guy's here."

"Good. Come on in." The voice was unexpectedly young.

Nudged by Yoki, I took off my shoes and went in. I took off Santa's shoes, too, while Yoki held him. Santa giggled as if it tickled, and as soon as he was put down he made a dash for his father.

"Easy, Santa."

Santa jumped into the lap of a man in his midthirties sitting on the tatami with his legs tucked under him. The man was wearing a dark brown kimono with a striped padded kimono jacket around his shoulders. His face was long and thin, and his eyes, unlike Santa's, were piercing.

"Welcome, Yuki Hirano," he said. "Glad to have you aboard. I'm Seiichi Nakamura, and this is my son, Santa. Please call me Seiichi."

Everyone just assumed I was going to stay and work for Nakamura Lumber. At this point, getting back to the station on my own was next to impossible. I had no choice but to sit down on the floor cushion Seiichi indicated.

Yoki seated himself cross-legged next to me. Then the door opened and a voice called, "Have we got company?" I turned and saw a pretty woman standing by the open door, looking at me. Her big, round eyes and clear, fresh skin were just like Santa's.

11

"This is my wife, Risa," said Seiichi. "Risa, this is Yuki Hirano, who's just joining us today."

"Pleased to meet you." Risa smiled at me.

My heart beat faster. Women this good-looking were scarce in Yokohama, or even on TV. Suddenly I began to wonder where I'd be living. This house looked pretty spacious; maybe the Nakamuras would be putting me up. And just like that, I was willing to generously overlook the fact that my employment had been arranged behind my back.

Risa made a pot of tea, and we all drank it. She served red bean jelly, too, and Santa and Yoki gobbled theirs.

"I was just having a look at the tea bushes out back," Risa said. "The snow damaged some of the twig tips."

"Yeah, it snowed a lot this year. How about on the mountains, Yoki?"

"The midsection of West Mountain is pretty hard hit. Lots of young trees there."

"All right, then," said Seiichi. "Tomorrow we do snow removal."

Everyone nodded, even Santa, but I was puzzled. Snow removal? The snow hadn't seemed all that deep to me.

Seiichi explained the terms of my employment. A monthly payday. Full social insurance. A typical workday would start at eight a.m. and end at five p.m., but depending on which mountain we worked on, the meeting time might be moved up to allow for travel.

The words *Actually, forestry doesn't interest me* were getting harder and harder to say.

For the time being I would stay with Yoki. What, not here? This was a letdown. Risa and Santa saw Yoki and me off, waving from the doorway as we walked back to the pickup.

"So what are you, a total beginner?" Yoki asked.

"At the co-op I learned to use the chain saw," I said with dignity.

"Pfff. The chain saw."

What was wrong with that? We walked along in silence.

Yoki lived in the house he'd parked in front of, the middle one of three lined up by the river. It was another old-fashioned farmhouse, not as big as the Nakamura place, but big enough; in Yokohama it would have been enormous.

In the front yard there was a red-roofed doghouse, and sitting in front of it was a shaggy white dog, whose tail drummed the ground furiously as we approached. A board nailed over the door said "Noko." Sounded like a girl's name to me, but the evidence in front of my eyes said otherwise. Definitely a he. I cocked my head, puzzled. Noko closed his eyes in bliss and seemed to smile as Yoki rubbed his head.

"Look out," Yoki warned as he opened the front door. The next moment, a bowl came flying out and grazed my cheek before smashing into pieces on the ground.

"Where have you been!"

A slight, delicate woman was standing in the entryway. She'd been waiting for us. She had an arresting, exotic face, different from Risa's. Here in the middle of nowhere they certainly had their share of good-looking women. Concerned about the smashed bowl, I turned and looked back. An old man happening by glanced from our faces to the broken crockery and grinned. He didn't intervene but went on into the house across the way.

So dustups like this were an everyday affair? Yoki, too, seemed unconcerned. "This is my wife, Miho," he told me. Turning to her, he defended himself. "I told you there was an assembly, remember? Afterward I went around on patrol."

"That assembly was *three days* ago. You expect me to believe you've been patrolling the mountains this whole time? Even at night?"

"Absolutely. Well, at night I stayed in the co-op office."

Liar. He never did. But I kept my mouth shut.

"You blunt ax!" Miho shouted. "I've had it with you!"

"Easy, easy." He held up placating hands. "Let's start over. This is Yuki Hirano, the trainee. He'll be staying with us."

13

Her attention was now directed at me, so reluctantly I stepped forward. "Nice to meet you."

Miho flounced inside without a word.

Yoki and Miho lived with his grandmother, Granny Shige, who was as round and wrinkled as a shriveled bean-jam bun. She sat motionless on her cushion, unimpressed by the hullabaloo. You'd have been pardoned for taking her for a mummy.

"Pay them no mind," said Granny Shige. "It's always like this."

She had trouble getting around, so she couldn't work in the kitchen. I stayed with her while Yoki went to fix supper.

"Miho called him a blunt ax," I said. "That's a funny thing to call someone."

Granny Shige laughed with toothless gums. "*Yoki* is another word for 'ax.' I named him that."

Then maybe the dog's name was short for *nokogiri*: "saw." Of course.

Yoki, Granny Shige, and I had supper there in the family room. The meal was just hot rice, radish pickles, and miso soup with wakame seaweed. Miho had gone into another room and wouldn't come out.

"She sure seems angry . . . ," I ventured.

"Nah," said Yoki. "If she was really mad, she'd go home to her folks."

He put away three bowlfuls of rice. Even Granny Shige had two. I was impressed that they could eat so much rice, with just miso soup and pickles to go with it.

Meanwhile, I was getting seriously stressed. I was going to live with a husband and wife at each other's throats and a granny with one foot in the grave, while working in forestry? It was insane. I'd have run away in a minute if I could, but the station was too far. Thanks to Yoki, I couldn't use my phone, and I had just a little over thirty thousand yen in cash. What had I stepped into? Mulling my predicament, I could only get down one bowlful of rice.

Twice a week, I learned, a station wagon came by for Granny Shige and took her to an eldercare center in Hisai for the day. Now she said she would go straight to bed since she'd had her bath already: "I scrubbed off all my dirt."

Yoki took her by the arm and led her to a room near the toilet. She said goodnight and disappeared inside.

The tub was old-fashioned, made of cast iron and set in concrete, a cauldron with just enough room to sit curled up in chest-high water. The water was heated by a fire underneath. Yoki explained how to use it, and I got in after placing a wooden board on the bottom to keep my feet from burning. The tub made me nervous; afraid of getting burned, I held myself away from the iron edge. There was no room to stretch out. I sat soaking in the hot water for a while, knees to my chest. Maybe because it was heated with firewood, not gas or electricity, the water felt soft.

Yoki went in after me.

My room was a six-mat room next to the family room. I laid out my futon and got under the covers, and then I heard voices from the next room, the one with the family Buddhist altar. Yoki was trying to persuade Miho to take a bath: "I'll heat it up for you, okay, honey?" He was doing his best to mollify her.

Before I could tell how she responded, I fell asleep.

Work in the mountains is generally done by teams of four or five. Nakamura Lumber employs twenty people, and they come from all over the village to work. Mostly they log on forestland in the vicinity. In addition to that, they look after the mountains owned by the Nakamura family, year-round.

Yoki and I were on the same team, the one that specialized in caring for forests on the Nakamura mountains. I would experience the full range of forestry jobs, from planting and managing timber forests to harvesting the timber. Besides Seiichi, the rest of the team consisted of Iwao Tanabe, who was about fifty, and a vigorous guy of seventy-four known as "Old Man Saburo." Both Iwao and Old Man Saburo lived in Kamusari district. They were veterans who'd been doing this work all their lives.

On my first day, Yoki got me up while it was still dark out, and I crawled out of my futon wishing I could crawl right back in.

On the low, round table in the family room were two big, shiny, triangular objects. They turned out to be huge *onigiri*, made with what looked like three cups of rice apiece, wrapped in tinfoil.

"Miho's in a good mood again." Yoki sounded happy—even though this was a poor excuse for a lunch if you asked me. Still, it was way better than nothing, come to think of it, so I cheerfully packed my huge onigiri and a canteen of tea and got in the pickup. Yoki lifted Noko onto the bed of the truck.

For about ten minutes, the pickup trundled on. Soon the road was unpaved, and there were no more houses. On one side of the road was a steep slope leading down to the mountain stream. The road got rapidly narrower and finally came to an end. Three other pickups were already parked in a small clearing.

From there we had to climb on foot. Noko, full of energy, went tearing up the slope through the undergrowth. Yoki strode up the mountainside with the same pace as when walking on level ground, his breathing unchanged. He carried his rice-ball lunch on his back in a *furoshiki* wrapping cloth; his canteen hung from his shoulder; and in one hand he carried an ax. An ax! I marveled. In this day and age, an ax!

Carrying a chain saw, I struggled to keep up.

Yoki wore a flat tool bag around his waist, kind of like the ones that hairstylists use. It was pretty cool-looking, but he of course wore it for strictly practical purposes. I made out various mysterious objects sticking out from the pockets, including a metal rasp and the end of a short piece of rubber hose.

The forest was dim, due to the heavy growth of cedars.

"This area doesn't get looked after right," Yoki remarked. His manner was gruff, but he did seem to want to educate me. "A well-tended forest is brighter than this, and it's got far more trees with thick trunks."

I was out of breath, unable to answer. When you actually climb a mountain, it looks completely different from the way it looks from afar. The incline was steep, and I had to constantly watch where I was going, so I couldn't look up. Sometimes it was like climbing the face of a cliff. Whoever had planted trees there was a regular daredevil. Foresters don't only plant trees; they have to tend them, and after they're grown they cut them down and haul them down the mountain—in this case, a mountain so steep you could hardly stand up straight on it. Unbelievable.

I'm not afraid of heights or anything, but the footing was so bad and the altitude so high that I started to shiver. I didn't want Yoki to think I was afraid, so I gritted my teeth and stuck close to him. We crossed several ridges. There were deep snowbanks in the valleys. As we walked along, sometimes a clump of snow fell from the treetops. Every single time, I jumped in surprise and ducked.

Finally we made it to the day's work area. Seiichi, Iwao, and Old Man Saburo were waiting for us.

"Hey there," said Iwao.

Old Man Saburo grinned at Yoki. "Yesterday, you and Miho went at it hammer and tongs, I saw. Did you kiss and make up?"

It dawned on me: this was the old man who'd gone inside the house across the street while Yoki and Miho were quarreling. He'd taken in the spectacle with amusement. Some friend. Why hadn't he tried to patch things up between them? Then supper might have been a bit more substantial. On the other hand, Miho *had* been steaming mad. Maybe he was wise to stay out of it. As I would learn, Old Man Saburo had an uncanny ability to sense danger on the mountains, too. The fruit of long experience.

"We kinda talked things over in the night," said Yoki with a poker face. "She came around."

Talked things over in the night? Whatever. Now I regretted having fallen asleep so fast. I felt like I'd missed out.

"Okay, now," said Seiichi, and he put on his helmet. "Let's get started. From here to the valley, row by row. Begin!"

As soon as he gave the order, we fanned out. They worked in pairs: Iwao and Old Man Saburo, Yoki and Seiichi. I was assigned to Yoki and Seiichi. Noko ran back and forth as if cheering us on.

The cedars were bowed under the weight of the snow, leaning heavily toward the valley. Some of them were bent so low, their tops were practically touching the slope.

"If trees are left like this, they grow misshapen and can't be sold for timber," Seiichi explained. "We'll get rid of the snow and fasten each tree to a shrub so the trunk can grow straight. We start at the top of the mountain and work our way down, row by row. That's the most efficient way."

These trees were young, but already a good ten feet tall. How were we going to remove the snow, straighten them out, and fix it so they stayed that way?

Seiichi showed me a rope of woven straw. "First we fasten this to a branch, right at the crotch."

Yoki tied one end of the rope around a branch growing from around the middle of the slender young tree. Then Seiichi squatted down and pulled hard on his end of the rope. The crown of the tree rose.

"Here's where you have to watch out," said Seiichi, still squatting and holding the rope taut. "You don't want to pull so far that the tree's not vertical and leans the other way, toward the mountain. If it's fastened at that angle, then when next year's snow piles up, the trunk will snap or be impossible to raise, and the damage will be worse."

He tied his end of the rope around the base of a shrub. I watched as the cedar sprang upright.

"Straw rope disintegrates and falls off eventually, so we just leave it like this. If you use ropes made with chemical fibers, you have to come around and get rid of them all before winter. If a tree can't bend under the weight of the snow, it'll break."

Urged to try my hand, I felt flustered. Yoki was moving on, tying straw rope around cedar after cedar down the slope. I couldn't stand there doing nothing. Under Seiichi's direction, I pulled on the rope with all my might. It weighed a ton. The trees were all slender, and Seiichi had pulled his up with apparent ease, even though he didn't look as strong as Yoki. I couldn't make mine budge.

"Bend your knees. Imagine your back is against the slope, and pull with your whole body."

With a weird-sounding grunt, I finally got the tree's crown to lift.

"That's the way. A little more." Seiichi gave instructions while lightly stamping the soil around the tree he had just raised. "Good. You've got it."

Careful to keep pulling on the rope, I slowly shifted my position and started to fasten the rope around the base of a bush. While I focused on that, my arm muscles relaxed a bit. All at once the tree snapped back, and I lost my footing and went tumbling down the mountain. In a panic, I prepared to die. Noko howled in the distance. At the bottom of the slope I slammed into a tree and finally came to a stop. The impact brought a cascade of snow down on my head. The ground was muddy, and my work clothes were now filthy.

"Are you okay?" Seiichi came running.

As I got up awkwardly, rubbing my butt, Yoki doubled over with laughter. The other two hurried over to see what the matter was.

"Looks like you're having fun." Old Man Saburo took in the scene with apparent envy.

Half in tears from shame and pain, all I knew was I *really* wanted to go home.

Toward spring, the snow is moist and heavy.

At night, snuggled under the covers, I could hear the sound of trees on the mountains breaking under the weight of piled-up snow. *Crack. Crack.* The sharp, clear sound, poignantly brief, echoed through the air. It was unbearable. I felt like I needed to jump up, dash off, and rescue the young trees. I could hardly contain myself. At the same time, I was overcome with sadness. Countless trees were planted on the mountains. I was such a slow worker, in a thousand years I couldn't have rescued all the young ones from the crushing weight of the snow.

As I tossed in bed, Yoki would get up and cross through the room on his way to the toilet. "Relax," he'd say. "Stewing about it doesn't do any good. Get some sleep."

He was absolutely right.

Working in forestry means accepting that some trees do break under the weight of snow. Not all of them reach maturity as planned. Those that break are living things, and so are the people who try their best to free them swiftly and skillfully from their burden of snow. Now, after a year in Kamusari, it's finally beginning to sink in that trees unable to cry out or move are indeed living things, and that the point of forestry work is to stand with them through the years.

But in the beginning, my reaction was completely different. Sure, when I heard the echo of trees snapping, I felt sad, but it wasn't the sadness of *"More trees breaking! God, what are we going to do?"* It was more like, *"More backbreaking work! God help me."*

My colossal failure on my very first try on Day One set me way back. After that spectacular spill, with Yoki laughing his head off, I fell apart. I knew if it happened again and I bashed my head on a rock, I could die. Terrified of the treacherous slopes, I couldn't pull on the rope with my back straight. Truth be told, I was incapable of handling *any* of the work. The knowledge ate into me. Why the hell had I let myself be shipped off to this godforsaken place just to suffer humiliation? I was fed up. Pissed. More than anything, I was mortified. My anger and frustration were just a way to distract myself from my utter uselessness.

In the forest, loss of concentration can be fatal. To stay sharp, we took breaks every two hours, and we lingered over lunch. One day we unpacked our lunches in a clearing where they planned to plant saplings once the snow melted. Gray clouds covered the sky.

"That'll be the last of this unseasonal snow," said Iwao. "Count on it. What with preparing the soil and planting, we'll have our hands full after this."

"Right." Old Man Saburo nodded. "Snow removal isn't everything, Yuki. You've got nothing to fear."

I looked down in silence. My skills hadn't improved, and as a result our team's working pace was still a crawl. No one blamed me, but that only made it worse. If I could just escape somehow . . . That's all I thought about. But I had no means of transportation, and Yoki alertly kept the key to the pickup hidden away at home. I didn't have a driver's license anyway. Escaping from Kamusari on foot was next to impossible. I could have tried hitching a ride to the station, but the villagers all knew me by sight. I was trapped.

As I bit into my giant onigiri, from somewhere in the forest there came the *crack* of a tree snapping. I sighed.

Old Man Saburo nudged Yoki. "Do something. See there? You're so hard on him, he's lost heart."

"I'm not hard on him." Holding Noko, Yoki scratched behind the dog's ears. Noko's fluffy white tail wagged, hitting my arm.

Seiichi didn't say anything, but apparently he decided things couldn't go on the way they were. One fine day after the snow had stopped and the breeze turned warm, he announced, "Today Yuki doesn't have to go to the mountains. Instead, I want him to prune the house woods."

On mornings when we would be heading into mountains nearby, the team gathered at Seiichi's house first to go over plans. We were sitting at the big table in the front yard, sipping tea. It was chilly, so Seiichi lit a fire in an oilcan, using wood chips, and we all gathered around to warm ourselves and loosen up. It's weird to take a break even before the day's work gets started, but that's just one more example of how the laid-back spirit of Kamusari plays out in everyday life.

"Us, too?" Yoki was eating a tangerine. I could tell from the sound of his voice and the look on his face that he was tired of having me around, that I was an encumbrance.

"No, you stay with him, Yoki, and show him what to do. Old Man Saburo, Iwao, and I will work on the south slope of Mt. Kusu, preparing the site for planting."

Old Man Saburo and Iwao promptly stood up, as if to say, *Yes, sir. On our way.* Noko's nose twitched with eagerness. Yoki looked disgruntled, but Seiichi's commands were absolute.

"Don't blame me if your cedars end up with a buzz cut." With that parting shot, Yoki walked toward the storehouse next to the main house. Noko leaped up to follow him, but Yoki said something that made him come trotting back with a look of resignation.

Seiichi and the rest each got into their truck, preparing to set out for Mt. Kusu. As Seiichi was warming the engine of his pickup, Noko went over and wagged his tail, so I lifted him and set him in the back. Then Seiichi stuck his head out the window.

"When you get more used to trees, Yuki, your fear will subside. Today you'll have a lifeline, and your footing will be secure, so you'll be fine."

Of course I wasn't fine at all.

The Nakamura house was ringed by a stand of fine old cedars called the "house woods," planted there as protection from winds blowing down from the mountains. How many generations of Nakamuras had lived in that house I had no idea, but it was good and old. The house woods were as dense as the woods around a Shinto shrine.

Yoki brought out the tools for the job: a wide belt, a stout rope with metal attachments at the ends, and blades called "pole climbers." The pole climbers fastened over our work pants and boots, anchored with a couple of bands to keep them on the inside of each leg. By thrusting the edges of the blades into the trunk, you could climb a tree with no branches.

But it looked hard. I put up some resistance. "Sticking these into the tree trunk will cause damage."

"The house woods aren't sold as timber, so scarring doesn't matter."

"When you're climbing the tree, these blades are all you've got to secure your footing, right? Doesn't sound very secure to me."

"You'll have a lifeline around your waist, so you'll be fine. Hurry it up!"

I went over and stood under a cedar on the east side of the lot. The tree towered over the two-story house.

I put on the belt as instructed. Yoki clamped the metal attachments on the rope to my belt. The rope went around the tree in a circle, fastening me to the trunk as if I were hugging it. Another rope hung from my belt with a chain saw suspended from the end. That way I could have my hands free as I climbed and, when I got as high as I was aiming for, draw up the chain saw and use it to cut off a branch. All that would be supporting my weight was the rope on my belt, circling the tree, as I braced myself with the pole-climber blades sticking shallowly into the trunk. Then, in that acrobatic pose twenty feet above ground, I had to get down to business with the chain saw.

No way. No frigging way was this going to work.

But Yoki grabbed hold of the cedar next to mine and scampered right up using only the rope and no pole climbers. What was he, a monkey? He had his usual ax tucked into his belt, and no chain saw.

"What's wrong? Get going." Sticking to the middle of the tree like a cicada, Yoki looked down at me as I stood there fidgeting.

I had no idea how to grab hold of the tree and climb. I tentatively put my arms around the trunk and tried to stick the blade on my left foot into the bark. The chain saw and the pole climbers were heavy, and I couldn't make much headway. Finally I managed to hoist myself a little off the ground. I felt like a junior-grade sumo wrestler practicing with a *yokozuna* champion. Outclassed.

The next thing I knew, the blades slipped and I slid back to the ground, grazing my chin on the bark.

"What the heck are you doing?" Yoki sighed and slid smoothly down his tree. He unfastened his rope, came over, and stood behind me. "I'll push your rear end up, so give it another go."

Unable to tell him no, I cursed my faintheartedness.

"Use your hips like a fulcrum, and bend backward a bit. Watch the feet, the feet! You've gotta dig in more with the blades."

As he peppered me with advice, I tried desperately to maneuver. Partly because he was pushing up on my butt, I managed somehow to climb to a point above my own height. It was still a long way up before there were any branches.

"Now you're all set. You don't weigh that much. Go ahead and climb. Easy does it."

Cautiously I moved my arms and legs, inching my way up. I started to feel like I was getting the hang of it. I saw what Yoki meant: with my hips as fulcrum, I didn't need to use my arms so much. Gradually I could tell the angle to stick the blades into the tree without looking down at my feet.

"You're doing fine."

Yoki was already up at the same height on the neighboring tree. His eyes under his helmet looked friendly. Getting praised for the first time made me elated. I was confident enough to take one hand off the tree and scratch my cheek.

"Keep it up. Climb higher, and don't look down."

That made me want to look. I started to turn my head, and Yoki promptly grabbed a handful of leaves and threw them at me.

"I said don't!"

The leaves struck my cheeks and fell. I followed them with my eyes and saw how high I'd climbed. My balls shriveled. *Get me down from here! Let me go home!* I clung to the tree and felt like crying. Only because I didn't want Yoki laughing at me again, I gritted my teeth and climbed higher, keeping my eyes trained up. I didn't dare look around and enjoy the view.

What branches was I supposed to cut? If I lopped off too many, the woods wouldn't offer the necessary protection from wind; too few, and the house would be cut off from the sun.

Yoki reminded me to switch the chain saw off frequently. If I slipped and fell with it still on, I could get badly mangled.

Following his instructions, I trimmed the top of the tree. It took me all morning to get that one cedar into shape. Yoki never took his eyes off me, but he still managed to shinny up and down tree after tree, working at five times my speed.

When we stopped for lunch, my legs were shaking. Hoping Yoki wouldn't notice, I managed to brace myself somehow and walk across the yard to the table, where I ate a giant onigiri. Besides the usual pickled plum and salmon, for some reason it was stuffed with a sweet-potato croquette, too.

"Wow! She must really be in a good mood today." Yoki looked delighted.

Miho's rice balls were like crystal balls, I thought.

The sun shone warmer and warmer. The air filled with all sorts of mingled fragrances: the sweetness of the clear water in the river, the green smell of grasses pushing up out of the soil, the scorched smell of someone burning dead branches. The faint smell of rotting flesh from animals that had died deep in the mountains in the winter. Everything was in motion, ushering in the coming spring.

The buzz of chain saws echoing from the mountains abruptly stopped. Seiichi and the others must be taking their noon break, too.

Risa brought us out some miso soup, loaded with pork and vegetables. "There's plenty more, so eat all you want," she said.

"Where's Santa?" asked Yoki.

"Playing out back."

"Oh." He seemed disappointed.

Warmed and heartened by the soup, we started on the afternoon's work. At first I was too tense—my legs shook, my hips were stiff, and I had trouble keeping the chain saw raised—but gradually I did better. The trick was to use minimum force and support myself with the principle of the lever. Press against the tree and find the best angle for cutting with the chain saw.

"Just because you're getting used to it, don't let your guard down." Every once in a while Yoki called out advice like this, but for the most part he left me to my own devices. I was starting to think he was a pretty good guy, after all. We finished the back trees—Yoki of course having done the lion's share of them—and started on the trees on the west side.

I turned on the chain saw and thinned out branches while below, Yoki raked up fallen branches and leaves. I dropped a small branch, aiming for the top of his head, and it landed with a thump on his helmet.

The third time, he raised a fist and yelled: "Knock it off!"

Then I happened to notice I could see right into the Nakamuras' house. By the window in a six-mat room there was a dressing table, amber colored, with cat's-paw feet. It looked old. A young woman was sitting there, looking into the mirror. I watched as she opened her mouth slightly and applied a light pink lip gloss. Our eyes met in the mirror.

Her cheeks were a creamy white. She was really pretty. Mischief gleamed in her dark eyes, where I saw myself reflected, and her glossy lips curved in a smile. She had the expression of a whimsical cat.

Completely distracted, I applied the chain saw to the crotch of a heavy branch that didn't need trimming. It fell, scattering leaves, and conked Yoki hard on the noggin.

"All right, you asked for it!" He let out a war whoop, tossed the rake aside, and grabbed the tree. Just like that, without any lifeline, he came charging up.

"W-wait a minute, Yoki. It wasn't on purpose, I swear."

He paid no attention. With frightening alacrity he climbed up by my feet and started ramming my butt with his helmet. I would have fought back by giving his shoulder a kick, but my feet had blades attached. All I could do was yell and scramble higher.

"Somebody was in that room," I said, trying to explain.

"What are you talking about?" He stopped head-butting me and looked where I was pointing. "There's nobody there."

The room was empty. A white cloth hung over the mirror.

"She was there just now."

"She? Was she young? Good-looking?"

"Um, yeah."

"Ah." He grinned. "I know who you saw. A ghost."

"In broad daylight? This early in the year? I thought ghosts only came out in the middle of summer."

"Here in Kamusari, they come out whenever they feel like it." He looked smug. "Seiichi's got kind of a checkered past. He broke some girl's heart, and now she's haunting his house."

"Yeah, right." I scoffed, but I felt my face go stiff. Ghosts and goblins get to me. A girl I used to date in high school once invited me to a horror movie, but I made up an excuse and got out of it.

We managed to finish pruning the house woods that day. In the evening, Seiichi and the rest came back. Just as we'd done in the morning, we all sat around the oilcan and warmed ourselves at the fire. The newly trimmed cedars rose sleekly into the sky.

"Well done, Yuki," Seiichi said.

I realized he'd given me this job to build my confidence. Old Man Saburo and Iwao also chimed in with praise.

"For a first-timer, that's mighty good work," said Old Man Saburo.

"And Yoki," said Iwao, "good job finishing up in just one day. That's not easy."

I began to think I might as well hang on a little longer in Kamusari and see how things went. Remembering how Yoki had silently bundled up all those fallen branches, I softened toward him a little more.

The front door opened, and we heard Santa's voice. "Nao, are you going bye-bye already?"

"I'll be back. You be a good boy and mind your mommy."

Out stepped the girl who'd been sitting at the dresser.

"You're telling me she's a ghost?" I whispered to Yoki.

He looked unconcerned. He was always telling stupid jokes.

"Want a ride, Nao?" Seiichi called.

The girl with a name like a boy brushed him off. "That's okay. I came on my motorcycle."

She rolled a big Kawasaki out of the shed and pushed it across the gravel out to the road. Who was she and what was her connection to the Nakamuras? I was dying to ask, but they showed no sign of wanting to explain. In a village this small, where everybody knew everybody, no one ever thought of making introductions.

"Nao needs to relax a bit," said Old Man Saburo, and everyone murmured agreement. That was all they had to say.

"What, she's gone already?" Risa came out holding a dish covered in plastic wrap and sighed. "I wanted her to take this with her."

How was Nao supposed to hold on to a dish while she rode her motorcycle? Then it hit me: this was my chance to get out of Kamusari. Sure, I'd managed to do a day's work for once. Everybody on the team had said nice things about it, too, and that felt good. Still, forestry wasn't for me. I was only here because I'd fallen into the trap laid by my mother and Kumayan. Hang on a little longer in Kamusari and see how things go? Really? What had I been thinking? That was close. I'd come near letting myself be disarmed by kindness.

"I'll take it to her." I snatched the dish and ran toward the road.

"Hey!" Yoki called, but I didn't look back.

Nao was sitting astride her motorcycle, letting the engine warm up. The roar of the engine echoed in the mountains.

"Here, this is from Risa."

Nao looked down at the dish I held out. "I don't want it." She put on the full-face helmet she'd been holding under one arm. Any second now she'd zoom off. I fidgeted.

"All right, then, I'll hold it. If you'll give me a ride to the station."

"What?"

"I've got business in Matsusaka. I just got paid, and I want to send my folks something. I've already cleared it with Seiichi." Just in case, I always carried with me the thirty thousand yen from my old man. That would be enough to get me on my way. "See, here it is." I took the envelope out of my pocket.

"It says *going-away money*."

Oops. Forgot about that. "It does? What do you know!" I tried to laugh it off.

Nao shot me a suspicious look, but then she said, "Okay, whatever. Have you got a helmet?"

"Yes."

I put on my work helmet and climbed on behind Nao. Was it okay to put my arms around her?

"Here goes." *Vroom.* She revved the engine. "No crying."

We shot off like an arrow, and I was almost shaken off. I let the dish fly out of my hands and clung to Nao for dear life. *So slender, so soft*—the impression lasted an instant. She was a speed demon.

"Aaagggh!" Terror made my eyes water and my nose run—but all these bodily fluids were whipped away by the wind. The mountain road was narrow. What if a car came? She pressed on the horn as she tore around a curve, the bike leaning so far to the side that my knee practically scraped the ground.

"Let me off!" I shrieked.

To make matters worse, Yoki's pickup was right behind us. He was holding the wheel in one hand and sticking his head out the window, yelling. He looked demonic. *Oh shit.*

Nao sped up, but Yoki hung right on our tail. What kind of engine could he have in his pickup? The car chase over the mountain road went on. *Faint and you're a dead man,* I told myself. Desperately, I willed myself to stay conscious. Even so, every fifteen seconds or so I blacked out momentarily.

The motorcycle and the pickup pulled in at the station at almost the same time. An old woman waiting for the train looked up in surprise. I got off the motorcycle and pointed myself in the direction of the station building. My knees were shaking so hard I couldn't stand. I got down on all fours and started to crawl, but Yoki planted a foot on my back.

"Gotta hand it to you, Nao, you're one hell of a rider."

"I had an extra load today, so it was gnarly." She laughed. "We'll do it again sometime."

That last remark was aimed at Yoki, and at me, too. Then she was gone, tearing back up the mountain road.

"You're a pile of trouble, you know that?" Yoki yanked me to my feet and shoved me in the pickup. The train left the station. Tears came to my eyes. Whether they were tears of sadness at having failed to escape or tears of relief at being alive, I didn't know.

"Where you from?" Yoki asked on the way back.

"Yokohama."

"Never been there. Is it nice?"

You bet it is. It's got places to go and things to do, unlike here. I started to say this but caught myself. Yokohama was also a town where nobody cared if I left. I'd sent postcards to my friends; I'd told them I couldn't use my phone and given them Yoki's address. Nobody wrote back, and nobody called on Yoki's black landline phone. They were all up to their ears in their new lives, no doubt. And my folks were so gaga over their grandson, they had no time for their son.

The possibility dawned on me that my circumstances were lonely and pitiful.

"Kamusari's no Yokohama, I'll grant you that," Yoki said, "but it's a nice place, too. You still don't know beans about the village or the mountains, you know."

"How could I? I haven't even been here a month."

"You really oughta stay a little longer. If you run off now, I'll tell your story to the end of time. All about a guy from Yokohama named Yuki Hirano, as pale and spindly as an enoki mushroom, a useless good-for-nothing. A hundred years from now, your name'll be a synonym for *wimp*. You'll be a legend."

"A legend in this dinky village? So what?" The idea was so ludicrous, I laughed out loud. Laughing eased my spirits a little.

"Look, relax. Don't sweat it." Yoki lowered his voice. "Nobody can do forestry work right off the bat. You'd have to be a genius like me."

The mountains loomed dark against the sunset sky.

When we got back to Yoki's place, the rooms were pitch dark.

"Miho, you home? Hey!" Yoki called out as he took off his shoes and went inside. I followed behind.

Granny Shige's voice sounded in the darkness: "Yoki, come in here and sit a minute."

I peered hard and could just make out her figure, hunched under the household Shinto altar. She looked like the ghost of a bean-jam bun.

"Granny, you're here!" Yoki pulled the string and turned on the fluorescent light. "Why you sitting in the dark?"

"You know I can't reach high enough to turn the light on." She blinked in the sudden brightness. "Your wife walked out."

"Not again!" Yoki looked up at the ceiling.

Granny Shige patted the tatami firmly, and Yoki obediently knelt at the low table. Somehow I felt compelled to do the same.

"What got into her?" he said. "She was fine this morning."

I thought of the croquettes in our onigiri.

"When you didn't come home two nights running, you said you were out patrolling the mountains, but you lied." Granny Shige's voice was stern. "You were in Nabari, fooling around."

"I was?"

Yoki played innocent, and just like that, Granny Shige flicked him on the forehead, good and hard. She moved like lightning. Before I knew what had happened, Yoki was bent over, rubbing his forehead in pain. The image of Granny Shige rising and striking like a cobra was burned into my mind. Maybe she was spryer than she let on. I looked at her with suspicion, but she was her usual round, bean-jam-bun self again.

"Yookiiii, won't you come over tonight? Puh-leez?" Granny Shige imitated a young woman's sugary wheedling. "A floozy from the hostess bar called here, and Miho answered. That floozy *knew* Miho was your wife. It was plain nasty of her. Doesn't say much for you, either, that you'd pick a place like that to have your fun."

Yoki listened contritely, head bowed, as Granny Shige issued this well-deserved rebuke.

"Until you bring Miho back here, don't you darken my door."

"Yes, Granny." Yoki got to his feet in dejection.

Served him right, I thought. After my escape attempt, I was starving. While he was gone, I figured I'd go ahead and eat with Granny Shige.

He turned to me. "Don't just sit there. You're coming, too."

"Why me?"

"If I go by myself, she won't come back. You've got to help me persuade her."

"No, thanks. She's *your* wife."

"I went to get you just now, didn't I?"

"Who asked you to? You came chasing after me."

"Idiot. Don't freeze me." (This is a Kamusari expression meaning "Don't be so cold.") He slapped me on the back of the head. "We're mates, you and me. We stick together, no matter what."

Dragged by this fishy logic, I walked down the night road with Yoki, glancing sidelong at the lonely-looking rice paddy, dry and brown, as we descended toward the river. Miho's parents lived just across the bridge. They ran Kamusari's one store. Beyond the glass door, on display in the earthen-floor room, was a miscellany of farming tools, detergent, food, booze, and cigarettes. They sold pretty much anything.

"Anybody home?" Yoki's voice rang out, and the wood-and-paper door between the store and the living area slid open a crack. The eye of a middle-aged man, presumably Miho's father, peered out.

"My Miho here?" Yoki said amiably.

His tone was familiar. Growing up so near each other, he and Miho must have been childhood sweethearts. Naturally he and her father would be on good terms, having known each other for years.

I couldn't have been more wrong.

"*Your* Miho?" Miho's father scowled and slammed the door.

"Come on. Let me see her."

"No. I won't have my daughter mixed up with a dirty lecher. She's getting a divorce."

"Don't say that." Yoki sounded pathetic. "Come on."

"I said no, and I meant it. No more mail delivery for you, either."

He must work at the post office, I thought on the sidelines.

Back and forth the battle raged on either side of the paper door. The wooden frame creaked as one of them struggled to open it, the other to keep it shut.

Finally Yoki took something out of his pocket and, holding it, rammed his fist right through the paper door. "*Now* what do you say?"

This sudden destructiveness left me stunned. On the other side of the door, Miho's father was silent, as if shaken. But after a moment, the door slid open.

"All right, I'll let it go this one time." He motioned with his chin for us to come on in.

While we took off our shoes, Yoki whispered, "I gave him a discount ticket for the hostess bar."

Sheesh. What a way for two grown men to behave.

In the living room, Miho and her mother were eating supper.

"Hi there, Yoki," said her mother. "You came early this time."

"Granny wouldn't give me any peace till I came and apologized." Turning to Miho, he flung himself prostrate on the floor in front of her. "I'm sorry! Please come home."

I had the strong sense that this was not the first time he'd done this. Miho said nothing, but kept on chewing.

"Yuki, you apologize, too," he urged me in a low voice.

"Why me?"

"Is this the new boy?" asked Miho's mother with interest.

"He looks young and full of beans," said Miho's father.

Since attention was now focused on me, I straightened my shoulders and sat erect next to Yoki, who still lay prostrate in abject submission. "Um, Miho?" I said hesitantly. "Yoki's really learned his lesson."

Silence. The delicious smells of grilled fish and potato salad filled the room. My stomach growled.

"Tell you what, from now on I'll keep an eye on him and make sure he goes straight home after work. So please come back!" I didn't have a shred of pride. The next minute, for the first time in my life I, too, lay prostrate on the floor, before somebody's wife. Hunger will make a man do strange things.

Miho swallowed and set her chopsticks down. I could feel her large, clear eyes focused on the tops of our heads. "Really, Yoki?" Her voice was husky. "You really won't see other women anymore? Because believe me, the next time it won't be a divorce. I'll kill myself!"

Startled, I looked up. With her hands clenched tightly in her lap she didn't appear to be joking around.

"I promise." Quietly Yoki laid a hand on hers.

"Don't lie to me."

"I'm not. And anyway, none of the women I've ever been with has meant anything to me. You're the one I'm crazy about, Miho. It's always been you."

"Yoki!" She threw her arms around his neck and burst into tears.

What a pair.

Her parents, clearly used to scenes like this, went right on eating.

We left their store, the Nakamuraya (apparently they were distant relations of Seiichi), and went back the way we'd come. The sky was so thick with stars, it was hard to pick out constellations. The gorgeous glitter made me dizzy. My having first run away and then prostrated myself faded to nothing in the larger scheme of things.

Yoki walked ahead of us, his steps light, and sauntered into the house. Miho, walking alongside me, murmured, "I suppose you think I'm crazy?"

Um, yeah not being an option, I said nothing.

"Ever since I was a little girl, I've always loved Yoki. Loved him so much I married him. I just turn to jelly around him."

What did she see in Yoki? Sure, he was good at his job, but he was irresponsible and reckless. On the other hand, I imagined that sharing a life with someone you'd grown up with, in the same neighborhood where you'd both grown up, could be pretty sweet.

"*Naa-naa*, Miho," I said.

"You're right." She laughed.

The first bit of Kamusari dialect I had ever spoken blended softly into the early spring air.

2

The God of Kamusari

Eventually the snow in the mountains melted away, and spring came in earnest to the village. The rice paddy was covered in Chinese milk vetch. When a warm breeze rippled the flowers, it was like walking by a pale pink cloud. Later, I learned, the flowers would be plowed under for fertilizer.

Tiny violets grew all along the paths by the paddy. In gardens everywhere, and even in the green foothills, countless magnolias bloomed like white flames. The sheer energy of spring was intense. It was as if a screen in dim monochrome had suddenly burst into living color. No special effects technology could possibly convey the brilliance of the change.

In the winter, the river had sounded hard and cold, but as tender new leaves began to sprout, the sound changed to a soft murmur. A school of transparent killifish cast shadows on the sandy river bottom, which sparkled like gold. When I saw that, I let out a whoop.

Spring made everything lively. If winter was like being under siege by a horde of Granny Shiges, spring was a hundred Naos tearing around the mountains on motorcycles—loud and energetic.

Yokohama had nothing like this to offer. I'd been thinking of Kamusari derisively as the boonies, but it turned out the boonies have a lot to be said for them. I would lean against the balustrade on the little bridge and gaze tirelessly at the mountains turning greener by the day, and at clusters of white spirea blooming on branches that hung so low they almost touched the surface of the river.

Now that I've spent a year in Kamusari, if anyone asked me what my favorite season here is, the answer would be spring. In winter there's snow removal, and summer is nice but the work is hard; in autumn, the food is good and the leaves are beautiful, but there's an insane festival that . . . Never mind, I'll get to that later. Anyway, spring is the best. Nothing can compare with the sense of excitement it brings and the sweetness of the air, filled with the mingled scents of flowers, soil, and water.

The only problem with spring is the pollen. All the surrounding mountains are planted with cedars and cypresses—huge pollen purveyors. Kamusari is menaced by an encircling net of pollen.

Little by little the mountain cedars began to put out what looked like brown fruit at the tips of their branches. I casually wondered at this, and before long the color deepened until from a distance it looked as if the trees had withered. Then Iwao began sneezing, and Seiichi began wearing thick goggles when we were working; he looked as unperturbed as ever, but his nose was constantly running. More and more village women wore masks.

The pollen attack was underway. That could explain why after my attempted escape, my coworkers accepted me back without a word of reproach. Maybe they were so distracted by their hay fever that they forgot to lecture me.

"Those brown things aren't fruit," Iwao said between sneezes. "They're the cedars' male flowers."

"That's all flowers?" I looked at the withered-looking slopes surrounding the village in surprise.

"Now's not so bad," said Yoki, "but in a little while they'll turn bright yellow, and then every time the wind blows, the branches'll sway and send out a yellow mist of pollen. *Swoosh, swoosh.*"

"Be quiet, Yoki," Seiichi said in a nasal voice, stopping him.

"Why? It's the truth. There's so much pollen it falls like rain. Pollen here, pollen there, pollen pollen everywhere."

"Quit saying that word, would you, please?" growled Iwao. Apparently just the sound of the word *pollen* was enough to make his breathing more labored.

Old Man Saburo, who seemed unaffected, took a deep breath and did some warm-up calisthenics. "You don't suffer from hay fever, Yuki?"

"No, not at all." At the time, that was true. I smiled, not knowing what lay in store for me.

"You're lucky. These days, almost everybody in the village has it. It's a real shame." He looked sad.

Yoki was disappointed to hear I wasn't allergic to pollen. "That's no fun." He, of course, wild beast that he is, could probably eat the male flowers if he felt like it and still suffer no ill effects. I'll just say hay fever is the mark of a civilized man and leave it at that.

Spring snow had delayed the planting of saplings. Now everyone at Nakamura Lumber had to work fast to prepare the ground.

"We're really shorthanded," said Seiichi one day, midway up West Mountain. "After we did clear-cutting here, we weren't able to come back and do much else."

"What's clear-cutting?"

"Felling all the trees in a certain area," Iwao explained. "Doing it that way makes our work easier, but it leaves the slope as bald as a plucked chicken. These days you hear a lot about protecting the environment. Well, with clear-cutting you run a risk of landslide. Thinning is more common now. That way, you pick out some trees to fell and leave the rest be."

One section of the mountainside, I now saw, didn't have a single cedar or cypress; it was a field, not a forest. Birds must have carried in seeds, because low trees and shrubs were growing all around. Unlike the artificially neat rows of cedars with glistening green leaves, this section had a relaxed, unconstrained feeling.

One small tree barely as high as my waist had clusters of pale yellow flowers shaped like little balls on the ends of its branches. The dark red stems formed a striking contrast.

"Pretty, isn't it?" I commented.

"That's elderberry." Yoki took his ax and chopped the elderberry tree down near its roots.

"Wh-what did you do that for!"

"What we're here for. Site preparation."

"That's cruel, cutting it down when it's trying so hard to live."

"What are you, nuts?" Letting his ax dangle, Yoki looked at me with disbelief. "There's nothing cruel about it! Preparing the site for planting means clearing out all the shrubs and junk. If we don't prepare the ground, we can't plant. And if we can't plant, we starve."

Yoki continued on up the slope, swinging his ax like a demon, chopping down young trees as he went. I was dumbfounded. Forest work meant becoming one with nature, I'd always vaguely figured, and here Yoki was hell-bent on destroying it.

"If ferns take over after a clear-cut, trees won't grow," said Seiichi. "By steadily planting trees, we protect the environment. Work with Iwao today and learn from him. This is his forte." He began wielding a long-handled sickle with gusto. He, too, showed no mercy.

Old Man Saburo picked up fallen branches.

Iwao clapped me on the shoulder. "Human activity helps maintain every forest in Japan. Cutting down timber, using it, continually planting more—that's how we take care of the woodlands. That's what counts. That's our job."

I wasn't fully persuaded, but I joined in the work. The roots of the cedars they had cut down were still in the ground. "Are we going to dig those all up next?" I asked.

Iwao laughed. "Certainly not. You underestimate the power of the soil. Those roots can stay right where they are. They'll soon rot and turn to soil."

Then I asked what would be done with the trees we cut down today, and he said they, too, would be left where they fell, stripped bare of branches. "The growth here's not too dense. Removing too much makes the ground dry out, and that's no good for cedar sprouts." He explained all this while deftly lopping off branches. I watched and tried to imitate him. My feet were encased in *jikatabi*, split-toed work shoes made of heavy cloth with rubber soles, and I was scared I might cut off my own foot.

"When we plant hardwood trees like chestnut and zelkova, we roll 'em."

"How?"

"Watch."

Iwao picked up a pole about six feet long, made of hard oak, he said; the well-worn surface shone with use. He stuck it into a pile of small logs, using it as a lever to lift them up, and began rolling them down the hillside, picking up others as he went and maneuvering the whole into something like a great big sushi roll.

"Wow!" I shouted.

Iwao handed me the pole. "Now you try."

Naturally, it didn't go well. The pile didn't hold together, and I couldn't control its direction, either.

"Once you get the hang of it, you'll do fine." Iwao comforted me. Clearly he knew his own skill was exceptional. His nostrils flared a bit with pride. "You see, we roll 'em down in bundles, and they form levels in the mountainside. Helps prevent landslides."

Then the small trees that got chopped down today wouldn't go to waste. They added nutrients to the soil and could even prevent landslides. I pondered these things as I followed Iwao back up the slope.

From higher up the mountain, Yoki yelled down at me: "Hey! Yuki! Don't wreck the soil! The topsoil's packed with nutrients—it's the life of the mountain! What kind of a moron walks along kicking up life!" He was yelling loud enough to cause a landslide.

Easy for him to say, I thought dourly. The rest of the team all walked easily along the steep incline in their jikatabi, but I couldn't. I tried to walk the way Iwao did, but with every step I took, the soil crumbled under me.

"Soft soil is the sign of a mountainside that's well cared for and rich with nutrients." Iwao was smiling with pride.

The mountains aren't only for plant life. They're full of insects and animals, too. As spring wore on and insect and animal life began to stir, I was under constant threat from all forms of wildlife.

The site we had been preparing was now ready, and it was time to start planting saplings.

"Tell me something," I said. "Do we plant them all by hand? Tree by tree?"

Yoki scoffed. "What else? It's not like planting rice, you know. No automation. High up in the mountains like this, what other way did you think there was?"

Alarm bells rang in my head. How many days would this drag on? "It's just, you know, such a big area to cover."

"Big? Nah. Two *tan* is all."

"Two what?"

Iwao explained the old measurement. "One tan is three hundred *tsubo*, so that makes six hundred tsubo."

Six hundred tsubo! The average house was built on what, forty tsubo? It sounded huge to me.

"We plant about four hundred fifty to five hundred trees per tan," Iwao said. "On this slope, that makes a thousand trees. Divided five ways, that's a couple hundred apiece. Nothing to it."

Nothing to it? I doubted that. I'd felt weighed down all day, as if I were carrying rocks on my shoulders, but somehow I summoned up my strength and started planting.

Seiichi seemed finally to realize that Yoki wasn't the one with a gift for teaching. He had Iwao teach me how to plant, too.

"If you try to plant saplings in a square, the higher you go up the mountain, the narrower the spaces between them, right?"

I visualized a triangular mountain and imagined planting seedlings on it in a square. "Right." I nodded.

"When the rows are too close together, the trees don't get enough sunlight, so we plant in a rectangle instead, with plenty of space row to row."

Iwao used a hoe to scrape away leaves and twigs from the soil. After that he dug a hole and piled up dirt around it, packing it down with his hoe. He dropped a cedar sapling about two feet tall straight into the hole. Then, after first covering the roots with fine soil by hand, he used his hoe to push the piled-up dirt back into the hole. Then he stepped on the refilled soil and tugged on the sapling to make sure it was firmly planted.

I looked on as he worked, admiring the smooth flow of his actions. Yoki, Seiichi, and Old Man Saburo, too, had all turned into human tree-planting machines.

"Here, give it a try." Stepping aside, Iwao handed me a big cloth bag containing saplings. I bent my back and thrust the hoe into the ground.

It went in with no resistance, and the smell of rich, moist earth rose up. A monster earthworm crawled out.

"Agh!"

"Don't have a conniption." Iwao picked up the slippery thing in his bare fingers and tossed it aside.

I shuddered. That was a part of nature I'd just as soon *not* become one with. I put on work gloves and focused on digging and planting, digging and planting.

The tranquil spring morning echoed with the sounds of hoes turning over soil, Seiichi sniffling, and Iwao sneezing. Now and then something would move in the underbrush in the forest nearby. Every single time, I jumped.

"Probably a rabbit," Iwao said. "There aren't any bears in these parts."

"I wouldn't say that," Yoki cut in. "A cranky old bear just waking up from hibernation could come this far. Wild boars charge at people sometimes, and monkeys up to mischief throw stones. Yuki here might even get bitten by a deer, he's so spaced out."

Just then Noko came running over in high spirits and laid something at Yoki's feet. It looked like some kind of plastic rope. I took a closer look and nearly fell over. "Gah! It's a snake! A snake!"

Yoki squatted down to examine the snake Noko had brought him. To his disappointment, it wasn't a pit viper. "Relax. It's not poisonous."

Afterward I learned that Kamusari villagers perk up when they see a pit viper. It's a poisonous snake, but they set about catching them with great determination. In summer, when you're walking through heavy vegetation, you have to be especially careful not to be bitten. Although if you ask me, in Kamusari it's the pit vipers who need to watch out. Yoki is always sniffing the air, on the lookout for one. They have a peppery smell, and as soon as he picks up the scent, he looks around, parting the brush. Around here they put live pit vipers in bottles of *shochu* spirits or split them open and grill them with sauce. Old Man

Saburo swears that grilled pit viper tastes better than rabbit, but I'm in no rush to find out.

"What's this, Noko?" Yoki said. "You killed a white snake! The messenger of the mountain god!"

Noko was wagging his tail, eager for praise. When Yoki patted him on the head, he looked satisfied and started to pick up the snake again.

"No!" Yoki pushed his head away. "You mustn't eat the divine messenger."

Yoki picked up the dead snake without a qualm and walked off, letting it dangle. I watched as he buried it by a big cedar stump. Noko looked momentarily resentful at having his prize taken away, but a second later he had forgotten all about it and was running happily around the mountainside.

We finished the morning's work and sat down together for lunch.

Seiichi filled a kettle with stream water. Then he started a little fire to boil water for tea. Food tasted great in the mountain air—even if lunch was always a huge onigiri.

Yoki broke off a bit of rice from his rice ball, laid the grains on a leaf, and set the leaf on the stump where he'd buried the white snake. Old Man Saburo filled a section of bamboo with tea and poured it over the stump as an offering. They took a moment of silence for the snake, holding their palms together in reverence. Even Yoki solemnly closed his eyes. Apparently he, too, was a believer.

"Did you find that strange, Yuki?" Seiichi asked, returning to his lunch. When I didn't answer, he smiled. "On a mountain, you never know what may happen. In the end, all we can do is rely on the protection of the gods. That's why we avoid taking life if at all possible."

Noko was intently devouring the lunch Miho had packed specially for him (dry dog food in a cloth sack).

The just-planted saplings rustled bright green leaves in the breeze. Misty spring clouds drifted across the pale-blue sky.

Thanks to the efforts of the human planting machines, the work was progressing much faster than I'd thought possible. "With you guys, planting a thousand trees really is a cinch."

"Dawdle and you can't keep up with the workload." Old Man Saburo picked up a twig to clean between his teeth. "After all, the master owns a lot of land—twelve hundred hectares!"

Yoki and Iwao nodded and murmured agreement, their expressions full of pride.

I drew a blank. "How much is twelve hundred hectares?"

"Twelve hundred hectares is twelve hundred hectares. What do you think?" Yoki ran a hand through his yellow hair in annoyance.

"Yes, but I can't really picture it. I know—tell me how many Tokyo Domes that is."

"Why do people always use Tokyo Dome to illustrate large spaces?" Seiichi asked.

Good question.

Old Man Saburo folded his arms. "None of us has ever seen Tokyo Dome, so how would we know?"

"What's the area of Tokyo Dome?" asked Iwao.

Yoki pulled out his phone. "I'll look it up."

"What! I thought you said there was no service in this village."

"There is on mountaintops." Scowling, he began to fiddle with the phone.

So he threw my battery pack away, and all the time he had one of his own! What a cheat.

"He's always sneaking in calls to his girlfriend in the bar," Old Man Saburo revealed.

You couldn't let your guard down around him. I'd have to tell Miho to confiscate his phone.

"I've got it." Yoki looked up. "The area of Tokyo Dome is 46,755 square meters."

"Which means . . ." Iwao stared into space, calculating. "One hectare is ten thousand square meters, so twelve hundred hectares is . . . a little more than 256 Tokyo Domes."

Two hundred fifty-six Tokyo Domes! I let out an exclamation of surprise.

"And twelve hundred hectares is 1,210 *cho*. One cho is ten tan, or three thousand tsubo. So the master's land comes to 3.63 million tsubo."

I cried out again in astonishment. And gave up. No matter what unit of measurement they used to explain it to me, I couldn't grasp the immensity of Seiichi's land holdings. I was floored—as much by Iwao's ability to do mental calculations as by the size of the land.

"I learned the abacus when I was a boy." Iwao seemed embarrassed by the respect in my eyes.

"Of course, the five of us aren't responsible for all the mountains," Seiichi said, getting the conversation back on track. "All the employees of Nakamura Lumber divide the mountains up and work on them. When that still isn't enough, sometimes I outsource work to the nearby forestry co-op."

"Not many big landowners do hands-on forestry the way the master does," said Iwao. "Eighty percent of all owners of forestland in Japan have less than twenty hectares. They divide up the mountainsides, and everybody gets a small parcel of land."

Old Man Saburo spoke up. "The mean ones won't give people owning land above theirs permission to cross their land. Then there's no way to get your timber down the mountain."

"I see." I wasn't planning on buying a mountain anytime soon, so the warning didn't seem especially useful, but I could see that land rights were a complicating factor in human relationships around here.

"Only three percent of all landowners have a hundred hectares or more." Iwao spoke with evident pride. "Now you can see that the master's twelve hundred put him in a whole different category, right?"

"Right," I said.

"And yet a big landowner like that spends his time on the worksite giving commands." Yoki chuckled. "Likes to work up a sweat. A real oddball. Kind of abnormal."

"That's enough, Yoki," said Seiichi and closed the lid on his lunch box. "People have been saying for a long time that Japanese forestry is a dying business. The days are long gone when a big landowner could just sit around and do nothing."

Over the course of time, I realized that Seiichi is not just a first-rate forest worker but also a brilliant forest manager. He's thoroughgoing in managing areas close to human habitation, where felling trees is relatively easy. With careful planning and efficient methods, if the logging cycle is carried out smoothly, even cedars thirty years old can be profitable. Domestic timber has slumped in price, making it quite competitive with foreign timber, which is expensive to transport. You just have to be able to maintain a steady supply in a fixed amount at unified specifications. Seiichi's vast land holdings put him in an ideal position to do just that.

In the world of forestry, a thirty-year-old tree is still extremely young, or as Yoki says, "puny." Seiichi, as a shrewd businessman, naturally had his eye on more lucrative timber. He is one of the largest owners of wooded mountains in Japan. In the old days, they say you could travel by foot from Kamusari all the way to Osaka over Nakamura land holdings. Almost the entire mountainous region from midwestern Mie Prefecture to Osaka, in other words, once belonged to the Nakamura family. The scale was immense. Their holdings shrank as they sold off land, but generation after generation of Nakamuras continued to work in forestry. The family still owned a large number of mountains planted with thriving cedar and cypress forests.

Cutting down cedars and cypresses from seventy or eighty to more than a hundred years old takes time, labor, skill, and nerve. Lack of workers means that all too often, there is simply no way to cash in on priceless old timber in mountain recesses.

Seiichi, however, set his sights on catering to a discerning clientele. He partnered with architectural firms and building contractors, guaranteeing them high-quality lumber. In other words, he created his own brand. The idea of brand-name lumber may seem odd, but people who suffer from sick building syndrome or long to build eco-friendly houses choose Nakamura Lumber even if it costs more. Even with the high unit prices, the company is swamped with orders. Seiichi's vision paid off. He won a strategic victory.

And Seiichi has a huge ace in the hole: Mt. Kamusari, the highest peak around the village, visible from anywhere. A sacred mountain where . . . Oops, I'll save that story for later.

Anyway, that day, having established that the land holdings of the Nakamura family were the equivalent of 256 Tokyo Domes, we ended our lunch break. After a few bend-and-stretch exercises to loosen up, we got back to planting, each of us with a bag of saplings over one shoulder.

Soon Yoki got a voice mail on his phone. The ringtone sounded weird in the forest. Was it the woman from the hostess bar? I'd promised Miho to keep an eye on him, so I pricked up my ears. I could hear Miho's shrill voice.

"Yoki, something terrible has happened! Santa's gone missing. Come home right away!"

We wrapped up work and got back to the village just after three. Risa came rushing out of the house and buried her face in Seiichi's chest. "What shall we do? What shall we do?" As if the sight of her husband had collapsed her defenses, she burst into tears. "He was playing in the yard. I only looked away for a minute, and he was gone."

"It's all right. We'll find him." Seiichi patted her on the back and spoke calmly.

The villagers were gathered at Seiichi's house. Santa had been missing since ten that morning. Seeing Risa out hunting for him, the villagers had pitched in. From the lunch hour on, the whole village had joined in the search.

Granny Shige was there, too. Declaring, "The master's little boy is in trouble!" she had come right away, carried on Miho's back. But there was nothing an old woman could do. She was sitting quietly in a corner of the big room.

Everyone looked sober. A little kid like Santa couldn't have gone far. Since he wasn't anywhere in the village, either he'd fallen into the river or he'd been kidnapped. Picturing Santa's happy smile, my heart tightened. Yoki, sitting next to me, silently chain-smoked. Mountain men mostly don't smoke, maybe because they're afraid of forest fires. That was the first time I ever saw him light up.

People took turns going out to search in small groups, only to come back looking dispirited. Finally somebody said, "Maybe we should report this to the police." It was Mr. Yamane from across the river. Then all of a sudden everyone started talking at once.

"Did anyone check Hyoroku Marsh?"

"Santa could never make it that far on his own."

"You can't rule it out."

"Don't talk that way. It's bad luck."

"Were there any footprints by the river?"

"No, stop! What about suspicious cars? Anybody see any?"

"If there'd been any prowlers, we'd have gotten word by now over the radio."

The village had a radio for emergencies, but mostly it was used for announcements like, "A strange car has entered the village. Please remember to lock up." That shows you how rare visitors are in Kamusari.

The chatter went on and on. Of course, everyone was worried sick about Santa, but I got the feeling they were also a little excited that something out of the ordinary had happened. Moreover, the missing person was the only son of the wealthy master. I sensed a little of the curiosity and cruelty of people used to an endless stretch of quiet days.

Yoki seemed annoyed by the chattering. He sprang up indignantly. "Never mind all this jibber-jabber. Let's go out and look again!"

"I'm sorry to impose on you all." Seiichi laid both palms on the tatami and bowed low. "Please help us."

A hush fell over the room. The villagers who'd been freely exchanging opinions now traded shamefaced looks.

"That's right, let's go find the boy."

"Master, you can count on us. Don't worry."

Saying things like this, they got to their feet.

"All right!" Yoki's voice was energetic. "Let's split up in teams so we can search more efficiently."

"Wait," said a gravelly voice. It was Granny Shige. "Tain't no use in searching the village. Sit yourselves down, everybody."

Granny Shige was the oldest resident of the village. No one dared disobey. We sat down and turned wondering eyes on her.

After working her mouth silently for a few moments, she said with great solemnity, "Santa has been . . . spirited away."

Whoa. An unscientific theory if I ever heard one. I felt like bursting out laughing, but everyone else took it seriously. Comments arose around the room as people whispered and nodded to each other gravely.

"Spirited away! So that's it."

"This year is the grand festival."

"Oyamazumi-san's festival."

"Um . . ." Tentatively I raised my hand. "What's the grand festival? Who is Oyamazumi-san?"

Conversation ceased. All eyes turned to me.

"It's got nothing to do with you," said Mr. Yamane. Everyone nodded agreement.

Then it hit me: no matter how much I worked and sweated alongside Seiichi and the rest of the team, I would never be the same as someone born and bred in Kamusari.

But Seiichi and Yoki didn't nod. Neither did Risa, Miho, Granny Shige, Old Man Saburo, or Iwao. If they had, I would have gotten up and left, walked to the station no matter how long it took, and kissed Kamusari goodbye.

Nothing to do with me? Give me a break. I was furious inside, but I didn't let it show. This was no time for hurt feelings. Santa was out there somewhere.

As if to cover up the awkwardness, Granny Shige went on in a louder voice: "Every so often, in the year of the grand festival, the god spirits away a child. To bring the child back, you must first purify yourself."

She sounded cool, like a prophetess. *You rock, Granny Shige!*

Seiichi sat up straight. "Bring him back from Mt. Kamusari?"

"Yes."

She said that one word and then, as if her work was done, closed her eyes and sat perfectly motionless. I felt nervous—was there some sort of village rule that a person delivered one major prophecy in her lifetime and then expired? I was afraid she had exhausted her strength, but her mouth was still working. Other than that, she seemed to be asleep.

Seiichi's decision was swift. "I'm going to Mt. Kamusari. Team Nakamura, come with me. Risa, get water ready for purification, and set out enough clean clothes for us."

Yoki sprang up. I didn't know what was going on, but I got up, too. The room buzzed.

"Master, is it a good idea to take Yuki to Mt. Kamusari?" said someone.

"Isn't it too soon?" someone else chimed in.

Seiichi quickly dismissed the remarks. "Yuki Hirano is a member of our village. What reason would the god have for rejecting him?"

No one could argue against the decision of the master. Mr. Yamane and others looked dissatisfied, but they held their tongues.

"Iwao, I'd like you to take the lead."

Iwao, who had yet to open his mouth, nodded silently. He seemed rather tense. Whispers rose again.

"That's right, they've got Iwao."

"If *he* goes for the child, then surely the god . . ."

People stole looks at Iwao and then winked at each other in assurance. They were starting to get on my nerves. If they had something to say, why not come out with it and stop all this whispering? My previous wounded feelings contributed to the irritation I felt. I still didn't understand the crucial role that face and gossip play in a small village.

Risa, her face pale and drawn with anxiety, slid the door open and stuck her head in the room. "The purification bath is ready."

"Thank you." Once again, Seiichi bowed low to the room. "Then we will be on our way. Supper and sake will be provided, so those of you who have time, please stay as you are."

"Be careful!"

"Come back safely!"

The villagers gave us a rousing send-off, finally shouting, *"Banzai!"* three times. Some of the women were in tears.

Jeez, you'd think we were soldiers going off to war. With my head tilted in embarrassment at this heavy solemnity, I followed my coworkers out of the room and into the *ofuro*. Located in the innermost part of the enormous house, it was huge, the size of a bathing area at a nice inn, with a tub made of cypress wood.

"Is this where you always bathe?" I asked Seiichi in surprise while we undressed in a dressing room easily as big as one in a regular public bath.

"No, we usually use an ordinary family-size bath," he said, swiftly stripping off his work clothes. "This one is for treating everyone to a bath at meetings and festivals."

The idea of "treating everyone to a bath" was amazing in itself, but I was no less astonished to learn that Seiichi had two different ofuro in his house. His extravagant lifestyle was like that of a feudal lord of old.

Water gushed into the cypress tub from three big faucets. Cold water. I had a bad feeling.

"Come on, Yuki, what are you waiting for?"

Urged on by Old Man Saburo, I stripped down, too. Buck naked, the five of us left the dressing room and stepped into the ofuro.

No steam rose from the tub. The water was cold, no doubt about it. On that spring evening the air was chilly, and I was soon covered in goose bumps. In one corner was a mound of salt.

All of a sudden, someone doused my head with ice-cold water. I jumped up in shock, unable even to sputter. Yoki was standing there with a cypress bucket in hand, laughing.

I found my voice. "Wh-what was that for? You want me to die of a heart attack?"

"You'll be fine. Look at Old Man Saburo."

Old Man Saburo, the most advanced in age of our team, was half kneeling on the floor by the tub, dipping up cold water with a bucket and pouring it over himself again and again. The sight was enough to make my balls shrivel.

"Is this some kind of ascetic training?"

"No, it's for purification." Yoki grabbed a handful of salt and rubbed it all over his body. "Here, you do it, too."

Why salt? I dimly remembered reading that people rub salt on indigo leaves to extract color. Feeling like a leaf, I shivered as I rubbed salt into my skin, then poured cold water over myself again. My senses must have grown numb. The places I rubbed with salt grew warmer from the inside.

For the final touch, we got into the tub, full to the brim now with cold water, and soaked to our necks. All I could do was laugh. I didn't want to, knowing Santa was missing, but my teeth wouldn't stay together. I couldn't help making a chattering sound that sounded like laughter.

When the purification finally ended, we put on white kimonos laid out in the dressing room. Like *yamabushi*, mountain ascetics, we wore a kind of white *hakama* or simple trousers, narrow from below the knee. I didn't know how to put mine on, so Old Man Saburo helped me. Crow *tengu* of folklore, half-bird spirits of mountain and forest, also dressed this way, I recalled, but with a little black box on top of their beaky heads. That boxy headgear was the one thing missing. Thank goodness.

Dressed in these anachronistic costumes, we went outside. The sun was about to go down. If we didn't hurry, it would be dark out and we still wouldn't have found Santa. The temperature drops suddenly at night in the mountains. We didn't want to run that risk.

Iwao sat in the driver's seat of a pickup truck, and the rest of us piled in back. Noko came running and barked, eager to join us, but Yoki told him no. "You took a life on the mountain today, Noko. The last thing you want to do is encounter the wrath of the god."

With Iwao at the wheel, the truck headed south toward Mt. Kamusari. Yoki, Seiichi, and Old Man Saburo promptly commenced banging on plate-like gongs hanging around their necks, using wooden hammers about the size of chopsticks. *Clang clang, bong bong.* The metallic sounds, hardly elegant, reverberated in the dusk. In the forest, startled birds beat their wings, and crows flying to their nests cawed loudly. The sound was so raucous it drowned out the engine noise. I covered my ears with my hands.

"Why bang on gongs?" The truck had just emerged from an old tunnel and started up an unpaved road. The truck bed shook violently, jerking my head so I thought I might bite my tongue.

"It's bad manners to go unannounced," said Old Man Saburo. "We're letting the god know we're about to pay him a visit."

"You do it, too," said Yoki.

Reluctantly I started hitting the gong hanging around my neck. *Clang bang bong.* Laden with this shrill racket, the truck sped forward.

We rode for another fifteen minutes or so and then got out and walked on a forest path for about twenty minutes. Finally we came to the entrance to Mt. Kamusari.

Beside a crumbling little shrine rose two towering cedars adorned with *shimenawa,* sacred ropes made of rice straw. Stretching on past them was a path so narrow I thought maybe it was an animal trail. It seemed to go on and on into the farthest depths of the mountain.

Santa couldn't possibly have come this far on his own. I knew it, but I couldn't bring myself to say it. This was their last hope.

People don't get spirited away. There was no way Santa could be on Mt. Kamusari, so far from home. But if he wasn't here, that meant he'd fallen in the river or been abducted by a stranger or was wandering, lost, in the mountains. However you looked at it, something awful had befallen him. But nobody wanted to think that. And so I kept my mouth shut and walked along, trying to make myself believe that Santa was here on Mt. Kamusari, safe.

Yoki and the rest seemed certain that he was here. Iwao, walking erect in the lead, and Yoki, still banging away on his gong, looked full of hope and confidence. Without even turning around to look at Old Man Saburo and Seiichi, I sensed that they were equally confident.

How could they be so sure? Common sense said finding Santa here was impossible.

Yet, despite my initial skepticism, as we walked deeper into the dense forest I started feeling as if Santa really were somewhere nearby. I, too, held my head high and walked on, banging my gong and calling his name over and over.

Looking back, I suspect that the combination of the cold-water bath and the salt rub, not to mention the constant loud ringing of the gongs, must have had me slightly tripping. Is that what people mean by a "natural high"? The steep mountain path, the solemnity of the sacred space, and the dense hardwood forest all added to the reality-bending experience.

That's right, unlike the other mountains surrounding the village, Mt. Kamusari wasn't planted with cedars and cypresses. There was a great variety of trees, all of them eerily huge. As the setting sun fell on the slope, rays of golden light filtered through the trees. Kerria shrubs drooped under the weight of yellow flowers no less beautiful. Rambler roses grew thickly, too, their white, five-petaled flowers spreading circumspectly. I caught a sweet fragrance in the air. There was deutzia, with an abundance of tiny white buds clustered at the tips of its branches, and swaying overhead were the branches of a Chinese flowering ash maybe fifty feet tall, covered with white blossoms like foam. Flowers on the akebia vine twining around an oak were bright purple.

Of course, at the time I didn't know any of those names. I was only struck by how pretty all the flowers were, and what a shame it was that with night coming on, soon we wouldn't be able to see them anymore.

The perfume of the flowers was so powerful, it was hard to breathe. My sense of hearing was sharpened, too. I used to think that forests were quiet, but I was wrong. There were constant sounds of leaves falling, branches swaying, treetops rustling in the wind, and birds calling back and forth, telling each other, "Day is almost done!" I could even hear an animal, perhaps a deer, munching on tree bark. From somewhere in the distance came the gurgle of a little stream.

The ground was soft with deep layers of fallen leaves. I could tell through my jikatabi how rich and moist the soil was.

This was a dreamlike place. I couldn't believe there was anything like this in Kamusari village. I walked along in a trance, all but forgetting why we had come, thinking, *I want to stay here forever.*

Eventually the forest was enveloped in a dim, crepuscular gray, and Iwao switched on his flashlight.

With that, I came to myself. *Come on, pull yourself together, man!* It felt as if we'd been wandering through the forest for a very long time, but it had only been the last ten minutes or so of sunlight on the mountain. We weren't even halfway to the top. My sense of time was way off.

Was it the magic of the mountain that I felt? I began to understand why even a roughneck like Yoki would piously purify himself before setting foot in this sacred area. The mountain's mystery, unfathomable by reason or the common sense of level ground, had me a little spooked, but at the same time it was pleasurable. The incoherence of a crazy quilt, the orderliness of spun silk: these two opposites were subtly interwoven in village life. I felt as if, for the first time, I had touched on what lay at the root of life in Kamusari.

Seiichi and the others kept on calling: "Santa! Santa!"

To shake off my surprise, I called, too: "Santa, where are you? We came to get you. Come on out!"

Then, just ahead on the path, a small figure ran into the circle of light from Iwao's flashlight. We all shouted at once. "Santa!"

He saw us and came running down the forest path at full tilt. "Daddy!" Yoki and I were both ready for him, arms opened wide, but he ran right past us to hug Seiichi, who was bringing up the rear. Seiichi knelt down and held his son tight.

"I'm so happy to see you, Santa. Are you okay? Does it hurt anywhere?"

"No, Daddy, I'm fine."

Despite this reassurance, Seiichi stroked and patted his son all over, making sure. His eyes were closed, and he was trembling with relief and joy.

Old Man Saburo uncorked the sacred wine he'd been carrying at his waist and sprinkled it over the ground. "Thank you. Thank you very much for returning Santa." He clapped his hands and began to pray. We all followed his lead. Before the majesty of the mountain at night, we could only bow our heads.

But how on earth had Santa come this far? Surely nobody would kidnap a small child and bring him all the way here to molest him. What had happened to him? I worried anxiously.

Everyone else seemed bothered by the same thought. As we trekked back down the mountain, Seiichi carrying Santa piggyback, Yoki asked, "Santa, how'd you get here? Whatcha been doing all this time? We were worried sick about you."

"Um." Santa rubbed his eyes sleepily. "A pretty lady in a red dress said, 'Wanna come play?'"

"A pretty lady? Who?"

"I dunno. A stranger."

"You're not supposed to go off with strangers. You know that."

"But she was real nice! When I said okay, we went *whoosh*, and there was a whole lotta flowers. Fruit, too. I ate lots and lots of peaches and persimmons and grapes."

Not the kind of fruit that was easy to come by this time of year. Yoki and I exchanged glances. Seiichi didn't interject but just kept walking in silence.

"I see." Yoki rubbed the spot between his eyes. "Whaddaya mean, *whoosh*? How'd you and the lady go *whoosh*?"

"We flew!" On Seiichi's back, Santa spread his arms out happily. "My house was small."

Yoki let that pass and kept the conversation moving forward. "Okay. Then what?"

"Then a lady in a white dress said it was time to go home."

This one had on a white dress, did she? I cocked my head to one side. Not that many women went around dressed all in white or all in red. Maybe one worked for the fire department and the other for a hospital?

However Yoki interpreted this, he seemed confused. "Was she a pretty lady, too?"

"Well . . ." Santa hesitated. "She was nice, though. The lady in red went away somewhere right away, but the lady in white stayed and played with me the whole time. She held my hand and brought me to Daddy and you."

Surely they weren't a pair of crazy sisters with a thing for little boys? Worried, I asked, "Weren't you scared?"

"No, no. It was fun." Right after that, he leaned his cheek against Seiichi's back and fell asleep.

"Santa met the daughters of Oyamazumi-san." Old Man Saburo said the words reverently.

"Yep," agreed Iwao. "Just like I did."

"What?" I looked back at him in astonishment. "You mean, you were . . . spirited away, too?"

"Keep your eyes ahead, Yuki, or you might fall." He waved a hand in warning, and then spoke as if tracing a distant memory. "How many years ago was it? One day I vanished, just like Santa did. The grown-ups ran around hunting for me all over, and finally they found me on Mt. Kamusari, laughing, they said. I don't really remember it."

"Yep, that's just what happened," Old Man Saburo said. "That was the year of Oyamazumi-san's grand festival, too. Forty-eight years ago this year."

"Is it?"

"Yep."

They were awfully calm, I thought. It was great we'd found Santa safe and sound, but how he'd disappeared was a complete mystery. Was getting spirited away really a thing? Hadn't he actually been snatched by a pair of pedophile sisters?

Those thoughts went through my mind, but the more I looked at Santa's peacefully sleeping face, the less it seemed to matter. He hadn't been harmed. He'd spent the day with a couple of strange women on the sacred mountain. Let it rest there.

Whatever strange thing happens on the mountain, it's not strange at all.

A big, round moon came out and lit up the night path as if watching over us. We didn't need the flashlight. The tree leaves shone silver in the moonlight.

Risa was waiting by the front door, and when she saw us she cried out soundlessly and hugged Santa, who was still asleep. Seiichi gently wiped the tears from her cheek with his palm.

The Nakamura house was brightly lit, and the whole village celebrated Santa's safe return with an all-night feast. Old Man Saburo painted a face on his shriveled belly and danced a jig. Mr. Yamane showed off his singing while Granny Shige clapped along, off the beat. Miho's parents sat beside Seiichi and kept him well supplied with food and sake.

Miho told Yoki approvingly, "You do make yourself useful sometimes," and he tossed back a cup of sake in good humor.

Iwao was sitting contentedly in a corner, eating. I went over, sat down next to him, and topped off his beer.

"Thanks. You have some, too."

"Can't. I'm underage. Tea's fine."

"You're awfully straitlaced."

For a while we sat there and watched people whoop it up. Santa had long since gone to bed. Maybe Risa had fallen asleep beside him; she was nowhere to be seen.

"Iwao, weren't you afraid of the mountain after what happened to you there?"

"Why should I be?"

"You were spirited away, weren't you? You might not have made it back."

"Never thought about it." He shook his head pensively. "Whether you get spirited away or not, a mountain is a scary place. Sometimes when I'm working in the forest, the weather'll change, and I'll barely make it home in one piece. But I've never thought of doing anything else. I've been blessed by the god of the mountain, so for me to live and die in the mountains is only right."

I was impressed. For Iwao, working in the mountains wasn't a job but a way of life. No other grown-up in my life had ever talked that way. He said it in a matter-of-fact way, too. Very cool.

Would the day ever come when all I wanted was to live and die in the mountains?

Toward dawn, the party broke up and we went home. Miho carried Granny Shige on her back, and I had my hands full dragging Yoki, who was pretty loaded.

"Honestly, this no-good husband of mine!" After Miho struggled to get his jikatabi off, Yoki collapsed on the living room floor. She gave his behind a little kick, but he showed no sign of waking up.

I was worn out, too. It was all I could do to make it to my futon. Still dressed like a yamabushi, I crawled under the covers and slept till noon.

Santa came down with a fever and spent three days in bed, but he bounced back with even more energy than before and was soon running around the village again, playing. He no longer remembered anything that had happened while he was spirited away.

"My head feels kind of foggy." When I said this to Yoki, he snorted. "You're always in a fog."

I developed a fever and lay groaning in my six-mat room. I kept on sneezing, and my nose ran. My nose and eyes and ears itched.

Hovering by my pillow like a specter, Granny Shige wiped the sweat and snot from my face. Miho made me rice porridge with pickled plum. There was nothing wrong with my digestion, so she didn't need to go to such trouble, but I ate it gratefully. I sneezed even while eating. My abs hurt.

It was hay fever. I probably ingested more than a lifetime's worth of pollen that spring. While we worked in the mountains, pollen rained down in sheets. Showers of pollen turned the mountainsides yellow. In the evening on the way home from work, we looked as if we were coated in panko and ready for the fryer.

Seiichi and Iwao were wrapped up completely in protection, with not an inch of skin showing except around their eyes, behind goggles. They wrapped their head and ears in a thin towel and then put on a helmet. Another towel covered their nose and mouth, worn over a pollen mask. They even wrapped their wrists and ankles to keep pollen from getting up their sleeves and pant legs.

"Everything itches," I told Iwao. "Not just the inside of my nose and throat, but my skin, too."

"Tell me about it. This year it's worse than ever."

Dressed like guerillas, or beekeepers, he and I commiserated with each other on breaks. Yoki, Old Man Saburo, and Noko were oblivious. They didn't care if it rained pollen or pitchforks. The inside of my nose felt hot, and my head felt so heavy I wondered if I'd caught a cold.

But I knew it wasn't a cold, because of the earthquake.

We'd been high on West Mountain, thinning a thirty-year growth of cedars. Forests over twenty years old get thinned roughly every five years, removing all but the trees that look promising for timber. Without thinning, woodland grows too dense; the trees get in each other's way and block sunlight. But over-thinning is bad, too. Cypresses die if they get too much sun.

Deciding which trees to cut down and which to leave is tough. You look at their location and the shape of their branches, and you leave the ones that seem to have the best chance. The idea is to plan ahead for when they are fifty or seventy years old. The trees that get thinned after thirty years' growth aren't entirely useless. While there, they protect the other trees from rain and wind, see that they get a modest amount of sunlight, and enrich the soil. And when they have thirty tree rings, they can be sold as timber.

I had no clue which trees should come down, and I didn't have the skill to chop them down yet anyway, so my job was hauling felled timber.

"In the old days, we used even the bark," said Old Man Saburo. "From April to September, it peels right off."

"Not the rest of the year?"

"No. In warm weather, the tree's growing, right? That means the bark's a little looser, more flexible. Winter's a different story. The trunk stops growing, and the bark tightens and clings fast to it."

People in the old days had sharp eyes, noticing a thing like that.

Old Man Saburo took a small hatchet and deftly peeled off a section of bark from a cedar log. From beneath the rough, gnarled brown bark, the smooth inner surface of the trunk emerged like magic, and the fragrance of fresh wood filled the air.

"We used to reckon how much wood we'd cut by the amount of bark left over, and get paid accordingly."

"You don't peel the bark anymore?"

"Hardly ever. It's not used for kindling now, so there's no demand. Besides, removing the bark increases the chance of the timber drying out and cracking."

Salaries at Nakamura Lumber were no longer determined by the volume of timber cut, but rather by the number of days worked. Of course, skill and experience factored in, too. As a trainee, I probably didn't make a third of what Yoki did. Still, I was glad to be getting paid at all. I wasn't getting done a quarter as much as he was.

Old Man Saburo and I carried the bark-covered logs down the slope and piled them up. Raw wood is really heavy. "Once you figure out the fulcrum point, there's nothing to it," he said, but I always staggered under the load.

To keep the bottommost logs from touching the ground, we spread out branches and leaves, and instead of using standing timber as a prop, we piled the logs up crosswise. They would remain like that for a hundred days or so to dry out, and only then, when they were drier and lighter, would we carry them off the mountain.

A slight distance away, Seiichi was choosing trees for thinning. He would peel off a section of bark to mark the tree. Yoki and Iwao put a rope around each marked tree, so that when Seiichi was cutting it down, they could pull on the rope if necessary to control the direction of its fall.

Deciding which trees on a slope to fell, in which order and which direction, is critical to ensure the safety of the workers and the efficiency of removing felled timber. Even Yoki wore an intense look on his face as he worked. Now and then Seiichi would ask Old Man Saburo his opinion. Old Man Saburo invariably made an unerring judgment and gave directions like "Start with that tree over there. Fell it in *oikoma* and the next one in left *komazaka*."

At first I had no idea what he was saying. It sounded like a secret code. Iwao explained that they were words indicating the direction the tree would fall.

Felling the tree to the right as you faced the ridge was "right ax," and felling it to the left was "left ax." There were eight possible directions. The upper right diagonal was oikoma, and the lower diagonal was left or right komazaka. A horizontal fell was *yokogi*, "crosspiece," straight back was *gombei*, "hayseed," and straight forward was *shomben-tare*, "piss-pants."

Amazingly, Yoki never failed to fell the tree exactly as directed. What's more, he did it with just his ax. It was a superhuman feat. A demonstration of true craftsmanship. Much as I hated to admit it, Yoki was awesome.

"Gombei and shombentare are only for idiots," Iwao explained. "Either way, the tree comes sliding straight down the slope. Dangerous as hell. Shombentare is the worst. The tree crashes so hard against the ground, it breaks in pieces. One of them hits you and you're a goner."

"A shombentare will make you piss your pants, no mistake." Old Man Saburo shook his head.

Iwao went on, "Unless there's something really in the way, you always want to make the tree fall uphill. That's basic. It's easier to fell the tree and haul it out that way."

I retreated a safe distance uphill and watched as Yoki swung his ax. Before felling a tree, he always announced the drop zone three times.

"Oikoma! Oikoma! Oikoma!"

"*Hoisa!*" we shouted back. This was a signal meaning "We heard you and we're in a safe place, so start any time."

With Yoki, we didn't need to worry, but if it were someone just starting out, there'd be no guarantee the tree would fall in the direction it was supposed to. Then we'd all be in mortal danger.

Yoki tapped the trunk twice with the ax handle.

"What does he do that for?" I asked.

"Yoki always does that." Old Man Saburo smiled. "Before he fells a big tree, he greets the god of the tree. It's his way of saying, *With your permission, I will now chop down this tree.* Also, sometimes tapping a tree tells you if there's a hollow space inside. With skinny trees like the ones we're doing today, it's not really necessary, but I suppose he can't help himself."

Yoki steadied his breathing and held his ax at the ready. Then, *thwock thwock*—the clear sound of the blade striking the trunk rang through the forest. The treetop swayed, and the tree began a slow descent, falling uphill. None of the neighboring trees suffered any damage.

As I was looking on admiringly, Old Man Saburo muttered, "Something's strange." That moment, the ground shook. I thought it was from the impact of the tree, but no.

"Earthquake!" I yelled. It was probably about a magnitude 3, but there on the mountain, it felt more intense.

"Get down!" Old Man Saburo pushed down hard on my helmet. Seiichi and Iwao were marking a trunk. Iwao looked up at the crown of the tree and saw the branches in motion. Seiichi yelled, "Yoki, run!"

Yoki had just started on a new tree. With a notch cut into it, the tree was unsteady, and if the earthquake made it fall the wrong way, he would be pinned underneath. Before the shaking worsened, Yoki made a mad dash up the slope, Noko bounding after him.

Just as Yoki came up beside Old Man Saburo and me, the earthquake reached its highest pitch. The mountain roared, and birds, unseen, sent up a storm of twittering. The tree branches shook hard, letting loose an avalanche of cedar pollen.

I thought instantly of the Sea of Corruption—that vast, poisonous forest in the anime *Nausicaä* that chokes all living things. *"The afternoon spores are flying . . ."* I never expected to see anything so fantastical in real life.

The roar ceased. Shining gold particles fell swirling through the air, piling up on the ground.

"That was a big one."

"Nice running, Yoki."

"Don't laugh. I was so scared, my balls shrank."

"Glad you're not hurt."

The men laughed together and brushed pollen off their heads. They were coated head to toe in yellow dust.

I couldn't speak.

Seiichi peered at me. "What's wrong, Yuki?"

I replied with an enormous sneeze. That was the moment I contracted hay fever.

By the time work ended, I was feverish. They took me to the one doctor in the village, and he gave me an antihistamine. The doctor was older than Old Man Saburo, and throughout the examination he shook for no apparent reason. Every time I sneezed, about three seconds later his body would jerk. I couldn't help wondering, *Hey, buddy, are you all right?*

Granny Shige and Miho looked after me, and thanks to them my fever went down the next day. The hay fever, unfortunately, is permanent.

And that's how I became a mass producer of tears and snot and sneezes.

"Pollen can't kill you. Let's go!"

Yoki was bursting with energy in the morning. Most of the team was suited up in protective gear, but not him.

Maybe it can't kill me, but I'm itching to death! Fog-brained, I glared at Yoki, willing him to come down with hay fever. *Get a taste of this suffering and see how you like it!* He never noticed the evil eye I gave him. He was in Seiichi's front yard, playing with Noko.

"This hay fever is a nasty business." Old Man Saburo cocked his head. "It hits people of all ages. I wonder why so many people come down with it?"

"Constitution, probably." Seiichi blew his nose. "Okay, everybody, listen up. Here's the plan." We were sitting around the big table to go over the day's work. "Tomorrow's the annual cherry-blossom-viewing party on the back mountain. So our work today is to clean the grounds and make a pathway to the mountaintop."

Cherry blossom viewing? This was a surprise. Spring came late to Kamusari, but even so, the Yoshino cherry blossoms were long gone. I had seen them by the path along the river, in people's yards, and in the foothills, shimmering like pale pink bonfires. How could there be any still left?

Doubt must have shown on my face. "That's right, you haven't seen the Kamusari Cherry Tree yet." Yoki smiled boastfully. "It's awesome."

"Why not have Yuki work on the lower half of the slope today," said Old Man Saburo, "and save his first sight of the tree till tomorrow?"

"Good idea." Seiichi nodded. "All right, Old Man Saburo and I will clean up around the cherry tree, and Yoki, Iwao, and Yuki, you'll be in charge of making the path. Meeting adjourned."

The "back mountain" was the low mountain behind Seiichi's house. While we walked to where we would be working, Iwao told me about the party.

"On the top of the back mountain, there's a clearing where a big tree called the Kamusari Cherry Tree is planted. Once a year, the whole village gets together there for a blossom-viewing party."

"Sounds nice."

"All you can eat and drink," said Yoki. "A free and easy time. Good fun." He added, "It's the one time of the year when you can talk to a woman without getting the whole village on your back."

"Just talk, mind you," said Iwao. "When Yoki was in high school, he shoved Miho down in the bushes, and it caused a scandal."

What is he, an animal?

"After that I made it right and married her, didn't I?"

Nothing to get puffed up about.

Yoki's cheeks were red. He and Miho fought constantly, but living with them the way I did, I knew they were still in love.

Iwao got the conversation back on track. "Viewing the blossoms is for everybody, young and old, but getting to the top of the mountain, even a little one like that, is hard work for some. That's why we make a path."

Thinned timber was used for the path. Trees felled during thinning on the back mountain had been left to dry here and there for use in the annual event. We would use those to make a footpath out of logs.

We laid the logs at a gentle angle of ascent, fastening them at either end to a nearby stump or standing tree so they wouldn't slide, and made a winding pathway all the way to the top. For people like us who worked in the mountains every day, the incline of this back mountain was a walk in the park. The log path was for people who had trouble walking.

Iwao and I worked from the midpoint of the mountain to the bottom, with him teaching me. Yoki did the upper half by himself. By lunchtime he caught up with us, right by the stream. We refreshed ourselves with cold, clear water and then ate our lunches. Seiichi and Old Man Saburo would be having their break at the top of the mountain.

"What do we do about this stream?" I asked.

I'd had a hard time crossing the stream myself on the way up. It was about nine feet across, more of a river than a stream, really. Here and there, stones poked out of the water, but they were wet and slippery. I'd lost my footing and stepped right into the current. It wasn't deep or swift enough to carry me away, but for a little kid like Santa, it would be dangerous.

"We build a bridge, of course." Yoki munched on his supersized onigiri.

"Out of logs?"

"You see any other material we can use?"

"How do we make a sturdy bridge out of logs?" I tilted my head, puzzled.

"No worries." Iwao laughed. "How do you think we bring out trees from high in the mountains? By chute."

"A chute?"

"A log chute, to use on a steep incline. We put felled timber on it and slide it down a thousand feet or more. It's a grand sight."

"Once the timber slides all the way down, you load it up, haul it out to the road, and you're home free," said Yoki. "Of course, sometimes there's a snag. A ravine in the way. Then we build a sledge road."

"We transport the timber by sledge," said Iwao. When he talked about forestry work, his eyes lit up. "Pile the timber on the sledge and pull it by hand. But first we make an elevated road. Drive piles in the ravine and cover them with a log roadway built like a horizontal ladder. A wooden viaduct. A sledge road over a ravine is the shortest route for getting timber off the mountain."

"We've made them a hundred feet high over a ravine," Yoki boasted. "So building a bridge over this dinky little river is nothing. We could do it in our sleep."

"Any time you let your guard down on a mountain, you're asking for trouble," Iwao cautioned. He turned to me and explained the traditional division of labor. "Normally, each team had its own specialty. There's a shortage of hands now, so we do all the tasks we can. Team Nakamura is basically in charge of felling timber. We're what they call woodsmen. Those like Yoki who work only with an ax are loggers. A person who splits the timber, removes the bark, and makes it into lumber is a sawyer. And there's one more specialty: those who carry the logs and timber down the mountain. Traditionally they're the ones who would make sledge roads and chutes."

I was surprised at the level of specialization. Each area required high expertise, which was probably why strict training was required. Would I be able to become an expert woodsman? Sharpening my chain saw was still a challenge for me.

Yoki uses a whetstone to hone the blade of his ax razor-thin. But hone the blade too thin and it will break right away and be useless; achieving just the right degree of thinness is tricky. At night when Yoki sharpened his blade in the earthen-floor entryway, I would observe, and sneak in branches for him to test them on. I told myself I didn't need to bother, but somehow I was always there beside him, observing.

I'd come to Kamusari kicking and screaming, but little by little I was settling into the life of a forester. I could hardly believe that when I first arrived in the village I'd kept thinking about escaping.

We finished lunch and set to work laying logs across the stream.

"See that stone sticking up in the middle?" said Iwao, pointing. "We'll use that for support."

They chose three pieces of thinned timber twelve or thirteen feet long and laid them across the stream, parallel to each other. Yoki stood balanced on them, trying to figure out the best angle to set them on the rock. It was like watching a circus acrobat.

Iwao and I piled stones on the bank, securing the timber at the corners so it wouldn't roll away. Yoki crossed over the newly built bridge and did the same on the opposite bank.

"It's better to lay the logs at a slight angle to the current, not at right angles," said Iwao.

"Why is that?"

"Think about it."

I looked at the log bridge and the stream, and thought. Then I understood. If the logs were at right angles to the stream, they would be subject to the direct force of the current. If they were at a slighter angle, that force would be dispersed, and the bridge would have greater stability.

"Okay, let's go." Iwao crossed lightly over the log bridge. I followed after him, but the logs rolled about, making walking hard. "Don't put all your weight on one log," he told me. "Turn your feet sideways all you can." I did as he said, careful to step on at least two logs at a time, and made it across.

Yoki was working on some other logs from the thinning, using his ax smartly. He first cut them in eighteen-inch lengths and then split them into two semicylindrical shapes. He laid several of those crosswise on the bridge and nailed them into place so the three logs were bound fast.

"Now you and Santa can cross the stream without getting scared," Iwao said. I was embarrassed to be lumped in with a little kid, but then, in the world of forestry, I was the same as a little kid, so I let it pass.

We made a log path on the rest of the slope, and that ended the day's work. Seiichi and Old Man Saburo came running like the wind down our log path. It struck me that they and the other Kamusari villagers just might be tengu, those powerful demigods of folklore who roam as they please in the mountains.

When we got home, Miho was stirring a huge pot under Granny Shige's supervision, preparing food for the party. The deep-fried tofu, a beautiful golden color, was for tomorrow's lunch. Unfortunately she hadn't had time to do anything about that night's supper, so we ate ham and eggs, the same thing we'd had for breakfast. But neither Yoki nor I complained.

The day of the event, the weather was fine. Miho got up early and filled tiered picnic boxes with goodies of all kinds. Then she made *oinari-san*, sushi rice inside little pouches of sweet deep-fried tofu. I helped. I filled the flavorful pouches with vinegared rice mixed with boiled, sweetened morsels of carrot, shiitake mushroom, and the like. I focused on shaping the rice mixture in perfect cylinders. It was pretty fun.

While we worked, neighbors called from the doorway. "Are you ready?"

"Go ahead without us."

Miho was frowning with concentration as she finished filling the picnic boxes. "Here we are, chasing our tails, and where's that husband of mine gone off to, I'd like to know?"

Yoki had sampled the drinks we'd be taking along, and all morning he'd been happily snoring on the open veranda. I didn't tell on him. When the boxes were ready to be wrapped in big furoshiki wrapping cloths, I went off furtively to wake him up.

The back mountain was surprisingly dense with people for Kamusari. We could see people here and there through the trees, climbing up the path we'd made. From the top of the mountain came the hum of voices.

We started up the path. Yoki carried Granny Shige piggyback, Miho carried the picnic boxes, one in each hand, and I carried five big bottles of sake, three in my backpack and one in each hand. When we came to the log bridge over the stream, we met up with Seiichi, Risa, and Santa. Seiichi was carrying a sake barrel and Risa was carrying tiered picnic boxes in one hand, a big pot in the other. Did everybody contribute food and drink this way? How much could they possibly consume?

Santa scampered over the log bridge, a lot more sure-footed than me.

The sake in my backpack weighed heavily between my shoulders. About the time I started to run out of steam, we finally made it to the top. When the view opened up, I let out a cry of wonder.

There was a natural space, carpeted in green grass. In the middle was a gorgeous giant cherry tree, more beautiful than any screen painting. A wild cherry tree. From afar, the innumerable white double blossoms clustered on the tips of the branches looked like mist. As I got closer, I saw that the blossoms were rimmed in the palest of greens, as if reflecting the foliage all around. The color was refreshing.

"Well? How do you like the Kamusari Cherry Tree?" Yoki turned and asked proudly. On his back, Granny Shige smiled toothlessly.

"Awesome." I could barely croak the word out, overwhelmed. The tree had stood for years on this mountaintop, its mossy trunk bending and twisting as it spread its branches to the sky.

The villagers were sitting around the tree with their picnic lunches. Beneath the canopy of blossoms, they helped themselves to the communal food and filled each other's sake cups. Someone spontaneously started dancing; someone else started intoning classical poetry. The atmosphere was free and easy, just as Yoki had said. People from all three village districts, Naka and Shimo as well as Kamusari, were there to enjoy the blossoms together in the glow of light intoxication.

Encouraged by Miho, I sat down on the grass and joined the circle. Iwao and Old Man Saburo came right over to share their oinari-san and other food. Yoki was drinking sake straight from the bottle. Seiichi drank cup after cup of sake, seemingly impervious to its effects, as the villagers lined up to pour him a drink. Each time, he returned the favor.

My being underage didn't seem to matter. The man from the Forestry Union saw me and came over. I had trouble placing him at first, and then I saw his huge biceps and realized it was Wild Boar Stew Guy.

"Well, Hirano! I hear you're quite a hard worker. I'm glad we placed you with Nakamura Lumber. That was the right move!"

His face was red and his steps were unsteady. He cheerfully filled my paper cup with sake. I rose to the occasion and downed it. Yoki saw me and said, "Have some more!" tilting the big bottle he was holding over my cup.

I started to feel really good and got up to walk toward the tree.

"You okay?" Miho sounded concerned.

"Perfickly fine," I told her.

I walked once around the tree. Roots of greater girth than the branches stuck out of the ground.

After I'd gone once around the tree, I nearly bumped into a woman. "Oops, sorry." I looked up and froze. It was Nao. I hadn't seen her in ages. Memories surfaced of her tearing down the mountain road on her motorcycle and me hanging on for dear life. The softness of her waist.

She addressed me, and my heart turned a cartwheel, pounding so hard I thought I might break a rib. "I heard you were in the search party that found Santa the other day. Thank you for that. I was away from the village on business. I heard about it later and my blood congealed."

Why thank me? As a resident of the village? What did she mean, *away on business*? What kind of business was she in? I wanted to find out. I wanted to get to know her.

"I'm, um . . ." I took a step closer. ". . .Yuki Hirano."

"Wow. You really stink of sake." Her beautiful face twisted in disgust, and she turned and left.

I'd just started introducing myself. She could at least have let me finish. Strength drained out of me, and I just stood there. I think I passed out for a while.

The next thing I knew, the sky was the color of evening. Someone had laid me down on a corner of the grassy clearing, and Granny Shige was sitting next to me. Everyone else was seated facing the Kamusari Cherry Tree. Old Man Saburo set a large bottle of sake at the base of the tree, took a stick with lightning-shaped white paper attached, and stuck it in the ground. As Seiichi reverently clapped his hands, everyone bowed their head.

"See what a good view of Mt. Kamusari there is from here?" said Granny Shige. "We show the god how much we enjoy these cherry blossoms. If we're happy, so is he. And at the end of the party, we thank the tree and the god."

Still stretched out, I twisted my head and looked south. In the distance, Mt. Kamusari rose high and clear in the evening sky. I looked back at the people gathered under the cherry tree. Nao was sitting between Miho and Risa. *You stink of sake.* With that, she had fled from me. There was so much I wanted to know: Where she lived, how old she was . . . whether she was seeing anyone. My chest hurt, but it had nothing to do with hay fever.

I sighed and looked up at Granny Shige. "How come Kamusari women are so beautiful?"

"Oh now, listen to the child." She giggled and gave my forehead a slap.

3

Summer Is Passion

The smell of water grew stronger as summer approached.

Or maybe it was the smell of rice in the paddy. A sour-sweet, moist, heavy smell, the kind you want to go on smelling forever. I never knew anything like it while I was living in the city. It's the smell of pure water coming into contact with nutrient-rich soil and young greenery.

I was sitting cross-legged on the open veranda, looking out into the darkness. A misty rain had stopped. Beside me, the mosquito coil Miho had lit gave off white smoke. There was almost no breeze. As my eyes and ears grew used to the night, the silhouette of Mt. Kamusari stood out, inky black. I sensed the presence of small, wriggling creatures in the grass and in the vegetable patch out back. Grasshoppers drying their wings, I supposed, and rabbits munching on fresh leaves wet with raindrops.

Thanks to the dense forest covering the mountains, monkeys, deer, and wild boar generally didn't lack for food, unless it was a particularly lean year. Therefore they didn't risk the danger of coming to the village to forage, and we seldom saw them.

While I was working in the forest, though, animals made their presence felt more than once. Leaves and twigs would patter on my helmet, and as I looked up wonderingly I would see branches swaying from the hasty movement of some creature.

"A baby monkey played a trick on you." Yoki laughed. "Not so long ago you were up to monkey tricks yourself, remember? Serves you right."

Deer droppings lay scattered on the forest floor, and I heard of people driving through the pass and coming across monkeys. But basically, people and animals lived apart from each other. The mountains were rich enough to make that possible. Then how come rabbits invaded our vegetable patch, you ask? In Granny Shige's words, it was "all because of Yoki's foolishness."

Rabbits are basically cautious and quick. Sometimes at work we'd see their paw prints or catch sight of a furry white tail in grasses, but seeing a rabbit up close was rare. A few years ago, though, apparently Yoki made a sliding tackle and captured one in the brush. (Again I have to wonder—is the guy really human? He's got the reflexes and hunting instincts of a wildcat.)

Yoki built a rabbit hutch in the yard using a wooden crate and metal mesh. He loved the rabbit and fed it cabbage and daikon leaves, but for a creature that had lived free all its life, this was a disaster. One morning it saw its chance and made a getaway.

"It never forgot the taste of the food here," said Granny Shige. "That's how rabbits started invading the village."

Yoki's rabbit would now and then bring its whole clan around for dinner in neighbors' patches as well as ours. But the villagers, easygoing as always, never did anything about it. "If those rabbits multiply any more, we'll have to put netting over the fields," someone would say. "Yep, reckon so," someone else would say, and that would be the end of it.

Old Man Saburo gave Yoki a piece of his mind. "You can't bring wild things where folks live! Wild is wild, folks are folks. Don't ever forget we're visitors on the mountains, or you'll earn the wrath of the gods."

After that, Yoki lost interest in making pets of wild creatures. *What's his hobby now?* I wondered as I sat on the veranda. He seemed fond of animals and kids, living things that moved in unpredictable ways, but right now all he had was Noko. The village offered no entertainment to speak of, so there was no way to kill time except by working in the mountains every day. Amazing that a guy of Yoki's vitality could stand it. Or wait, maybe that's why he went to the hostess bar in Nabari: because he *couldn't* stand it.

I was bored, too. I had so much time on my hands at night. The TV had hardly any channels. I would sharpen the chain saw, and then from supper till bedtime, there was nothing to do. Bo-ring! I wanted to shout it till it echoed: *BO-RING!!*

Rainy season in the mountains is especially depressing. The weather gets unbelievably damp and humid. Fog rolls in from all sides, and there's a chill in the air. Wet laundry doesn't dry. We had to keep a fire going in the family room and hang stuff to dry there, work clothes and underwear, you name it. Eating underneath Miho's bras was super-awkward. And Granny Shige's drawers—I seriously did not need to see that.

In Kamusari village the mountains normally block sunlight for a good portion of the day anyway, but in the rainy season you almost forget there even *is* a sun. It's so gloomy and dark, you start wondering if you're in midwinter Siberia.

So there I was, zoning out on the veranda for a change of scenery. The hateful fog hung over the Kamusari River that evening and didn't seep into the village. Visibility was good. Dense rain clouds still covered the sky, but seeing the black outline of the Kamusari range for the first time in a long while was kind of restful.

Something moist touched my bare toes. Noko had put his front paws up on the veranda and stuck his nose against my foot.

"Hey, don't smell my feet!"

I drew my leg back and patted him on the head. Noko jumped up beside me. He climbed on my thigh and licked my cheek. In return I put my arm around him and scratched his back, and that made him wag his tail so hard it seemed it might fly off.

A cute, smart dog. The complete opposite of its owner.

The sound of a truck's engine came from the bridge, and headlights lit up the tree in the yard. Noko jumped down off the veranda and ran to the front gate. The truck pulled up in the driveway with a few toots of the horn. Yoki got out and went around to the passenger side, with Noko clamoring at his feet. So Noko liked Yoki best, after all. The sudden absence of the dog's warmth left me feeling lonesome and bereft.

I sighed. How long had it been since I even talked to a girl? I hadn't taken a monk's vows that I could recall, but somehow my life had taken an all-too-ascetic turn. It wasn't only the constant rain that had me down, and I knew it. Ever since the cherry-blossom-viewing party, I'd thought of nothing but Nao. But I was too afraid of being teased to let on to anyone.

I brushed away my distress and stood up. Yoki had just hoisted Granny Shige from the passenger seat onto his back. Then I remembered: he'd said he was going to pick her up from the eldercare center on his way home from buying tools.

"Welcome back."

"Oh, Yuki. Great. Come with us a minute," said Yoki. His hands were full, so it was Granny Shige who beckoned to me from her perch on his back.

"What for?"

"Fireflies in the paddy yonder, the first this year."

"What?"

Yoki headed back toward the front gate, with Granny Shige riding piggyback. I ran inside the house, cut across the family room, and slipped on rubber sandals in the entryway. I called to Miho, who was washing up in the kitchen.

"Miho, there are fireflies! Let's go see them!"

"Fireflies?"

My enthusiasm took her by surprise. I grabbed her by the hand, turned off the faucet while I was at it, and ran with her to the front door. Yoki was standing in the road in front of the house, waiting. Noko was there, too.

"Oh, you're back!" Miho said. "Granny, how was your day?"

"I had a nice bath." She always looked forward to her bath during her days out of the house. "But you know old Mr. Murata from Shimo district? He hasn't got long now. Wasn't there again today."

"He was doing so well in the spring."

"He's over the hill. That's just how it goes. There'll be a funeral, mark my words, so get ready."

"Right."

Hard to tell if they were being brutal or accepting the inevitable in a matter-of-fact way, I thought, listening to this calm exchange. In this village where more people died than were born, maybe you couldn't get along without the fortitude and determination to combine Kamusari nonchalance with a dose of *That's just how it goes.*

"Over here!" Yoki said, walking toward the paddy by the river.

The road was almost pitch black, lit only by orange security lights and the faint glow from under the eaves of houses along the way. As the road sloped downhill, the smell of water grew stronger, and the sounds of the river accentuated the silence. The darkness was so deep, I got a little scared. I felt as if the surrounding mountains were weighing down on us, and the invisibly murmuring river would gradually rise, fog and all, and engulf us.

"Look!" Yoki pointed.

Straining my eyes, I made out faint points of light. Tiny greenish-yellow lights were flitting back and forth over the paddy.

"So pretty," said Miho. "I never get tired of seeing them." She sounded entranced.

"I never saw any before," I said.

"Never?" Yoki sounded startled. "Not just this year—you mean never ever?"

"That's right."

Fireflies—ones appearing naturally like this—don't exist where I grew up. They were mysterious to me. I put my face up close to one that had come to rest on a nearby rice stalk. When it emitted its faint light, the figure of the little black insect was momentarily revealed. Its rear end really did light up. The light soon melted into the darkness and then shone again. Firefly light was of a color and quality I had never seen before, different from flame or electricity or stars or the moon or the sun. It was fuzzy in outline. I couldn't imagine what temperature it would be if I touched it. It looked cold, but it also looked as if it might burn. All around the paddy, such lights were floating and fading and floating again, bringing a dim glow to the night.

My fear had vanished.

"These are Heike fireflies," Yoki told me. "There'll be more and more of them now. Yep, this is the season for love."

I gave him a sidelong glance. He was grinning. The guy was onto me. He could smell romance a mile away.

"The phone's ringing!" said Miho. "It's ours." She scurried off home. Amazingly good hearing.

Yoki, Granny Shige, and I wound up our firefly outing and started back.

"Say, Yuki. Isn't there something you've been wanting to ask me?" Yoki said.

"Yes, actually. I'd like to know what your hobby is."

"Don't try to fool me."

"No, I mean it. Like, it rains all the time, and after work there's nothing to do. What do you do to pass the time?"

"Well, I'll tell you . . ." He measured the distance from Miho's back in the road ahead, and lowered his voice. "I fool around on the side."

"*That's* your hobby?" Just what I'd thought, but I was disgusted all the same. "You mean the hostess bar in Nabari?"

"There's a place in Nagoya I go to, too, when I'm selling timber there." He gave a self-satisfied chuckle, and Granny Shige, riding on his back, smacked him on the head.

"She can hear you!"

Yoki's way of spending his free time was of no help to me whatsoever. And I still wasn't able to bring up what was really weighing on my mind: Nao. The whole conversation had been a waste of breath.

"But hey," said Yoki, "you've come a long way. Imagine that—you with time on your hands."

He was right. In the spring, before I could wonder what to do with myself after work, I used to crash. But now I had stamina, and I'd grown used to village life.

Could and should a guy my age get used to living somewhere with no magazines to read or clothes to buy? I used to wonder this, but it turned out to be no big deal. Those things are pretty easy to do without. As you can tell from the way I let myself be forced into coming here in the first place, I don't have much spirit of resistance. Maybe it's just too much trouble, or maybe I'm adaptable. You can't really call it right or wrong, I think.

Oops, I got offtrack. Anyway, Yoki, Granny Shige, and I went back to the house in the damp night air.

When we walked in, Miho was just setting the receiver down.

"Old Mr. Murata died," she said quietly.

Unless there's a real downpour, forestry work goes on as usual. All through the rainy season, our team went into the mountains and worked. From the end of June, we mainly cleared weeds. With the rising temperature and plentiful rainfall, weeds were rampant on the mountainsides, especially on West Mountain, where we'd just planted saplings in the spring. Unless we did something, the weeds would grow so aggressively that they'd throttle the young cedars and stunt their growth. So until the young cedars reached a certain height, we cleared weeds twice, once in June and again in August. In a forest of tall cedars, just August was enough, I learned. Even then, we had to hustle. Clearing weeds at least once a year meant covering all the mountains, a mind-boggling task. Forestry work is really time-consuming, yet it's so unprofitable that the industry is in decline. But without maintenance, timber forests degenerate. And you can't do the work unless you love it.

"Planting trees protects the environment. That's how city folks think," said Iwao. Now that the pollen season had ended, he climbed West Mountain happily. It was still drizzling, and the footing was bad, but he didn't seem to mind. "Forests produce oxygen, they say, but trees are also living things. They breathe. So of course they produce carbon dioxide as well."

"Yes, they must, now that you mention it."

I had vaguely thought that plants just took in carbon dioxide and released oxygen. But during photosynthesis, they do the other kind of breathing, too, taking in oxygen and releasing carbon dioxide.

"You can't go around planting trees wherever you feel like it and then just forget about them," said Iwao. "You've got to think in terms of the cycle. Not doing any maintenance, just letting things go—that's not 'nature.' You've got to help the cycle along, keep the mountain in shape, and *that's* how you preserve nature." He began cutting grass with a big scythe. "So, Yuki, I don't want to hear you say anything daft like, 'Oh, the poor weeds!'" He changed the inflection of his voice, mocking me. He'd never forgotten my reaction when we thinned the forest.

"Not likely." Offended, I raised my scythe, too. "By the way, what about the man who died, Mr. Murata, was it? Aren't we going to the funeral?"

"It was so sudden. I never thought he was in that bad a way." Iwao's shoulders slumped. "I'm going to knock off early today and go to the wake."

"We'll all go to the funeral tomorrow," said Seiichi. "Do you have mourning clothes, Yuki?"

I hadn't brought anything but everyday clothes. My school uniform wouldn't be appropriate, since I'd graduated, and there wasn't time to phone home and order something.

"I'll let you borrow a suit of mine and a Buddhist rosary," Seiichi offered.

You were supposed to take what they called "incense money" to a funeral, I remembered. *How much?* I wondered. Dealing with such questions on my own made me conscious that in society's eyes I was now a full-fledged adult.

According to Seiichi and the rest of the team, there was a community fund for weddings, funerals, and other ceremonial occasions, which everyone chipped in to, depending on the district where they lived. I had never met the late Mr. Murata, but apparently he'd lived in the lowland Shimo district, which since yesterday had been in a whirl of preparations for his wake and funeral. The women were busy cooking while the men built a temporary altar, arranged for a casket, and so on. Since I lived in Kamusari district, all I needed to do was show up.

A thin fog crept up from the valley and flowed around our feet.

We formed a line and scythed the grasses, working our way uphill. The long-handled scythe came up to my biceps. Not having to bend over lessened the physical toll but made the thing awkward to handle.

Yoki swung away with practiced ease. He looked like the grim reaper. Neatly avoiding the cedar saplings, he steadily mowed down the thick overgrowth.

Pretty soon I was lagging behind the others.

"Take your time." Seiichi looked back at me. "Don't cut your foot."

The minute he said that, the blade of my scythe slipped, and I cut down one of the precious cedar saplings. *Uh-oh.* I crouched down and stuck the end of the little tree in the ground, wondering if cuttings grew roots. Didn't seem likely. I wasn't going to fool anyone.

Sensing someone behind me, I turned around and looked up. Yoki was standing there wrathfully, feet apart. At a time like this, he was sharp-sighted.

"You dope!" His angry roar echoed against the hillside. "What kind of a moron chops down the source of his livelihood!"

I shrank into myself. "Sorry!" Not that apologizing would bring back the sapling.

"Relax," Old Man Saburo soothed.

Iwao came down the hillside. "It's his first time. He couldn't help it." Turning to me, he said, "Here's what you do when you're mowing weeds near a sapling. First, you set the blade facing up, alongside the tree root. Bear down on the handle and push into the weeds." He put his hands over mine and showed me. "Once you're in, turn the blade down, facing out, and draw it back. See? That way you won't touch the cedars. You'll only cut weeds."

"Okay."

After I got the hang of it, my spirits recovered and I set to work again. Iwao stayed a while to watch and then clapped me on the shoulder. "That's the way." He went back to his spot. Yoki went on glaring at me like the grim reaper.

All right already. I won't do it again, okay?

With the rain and fog and sweat, my work clothes started to feel wet and heavy. If I stopped working for a second, heat leached from my body, and I felt a chill. At lunchtime, we made a fire. The trees around us were enveloped in fine mist, while peaks in the distance were shrouded in white clouds. The thin fog crept steadily higher as we watched.

"I think we'd all better knock off early today." Seiichi put out the fire and carefully covered the ashes in dirt.

We had finished cutting all the weeds halfway up the mountain, and we'd gone quite a bit higher than that, too.

"It's the descent of the gods." Old Man Saburo's voice was tense.

I stopped swinging the scythe. Yoki was looking over at Mt. Kamusari, where starting at the peak, an avalanche of white cloud was sliding down the mountain. No, not cloud—fog. Thick fog was surging down the mountainside like a great wave, approaching the village in the blink of an eye.

Wordlessly, we all gathered around Seiichi. Yoki softly called, "Noko!" The dog came bounding down the mountainside. I might have imagined it, but his tail seemed wound a little tighter than usual.

"What's the descent of the gods?" I asked in a small voice.

"It's when fog rolls down Mt. Kamusari," Seiichi said. "Once it happens there, it starts on the surrounding mountains, too."

Before he finished speaking, there on West Mountain where we were, something changed. Until then a light fog had been creeping up from the valley, but in a heartbeat its motion stopped and milk-white fog came cascading down from the summit.

"Ah!" The next instant, I was engulfed in white. Seiichi and Yoki had been standing right by me, but I couldn't see them anymore. The fog swallowed all sound. I wasn't even sure if I was standing on solid ground. I started to panic.

"Quiet," Seiichi whispered. "It's all right. Hold still."

I gripped the handle of the scythe, its blade firmly against the ground. *I'm all right. I'm here.* I controlled my breathing and calmed my nerves.

Boom. Boom. A low, muffled sound like the beating of a big drum came from Mt. Kamusari, followed by the faint tinkle of a bell. I thought I was hearing things, but no—a soft *ting-a-ling* descended from the summit and passed me by. I was petrified, unable to move a muscle.

The tinkling sound disappeared toward the valley, and after a short interval the fog, which had begun to seem a permanent fixture, dissipated.

We all let out our breath at the same time. It was as if we'd been paralyzed. The fog lifted, and I could see everyone's faces. While the fog was thick I hadn't felt their presence at all, but they were standing closer to me than I'd imagined.

"What was that?" I asked in a daze.

"Like the man said, the descent of the gods." Yoki sounded like his old self.

Iwao moved his shoulders up and down to loosen them. "You mustn't talk during it. The gods on all the mountains in Kamusari go out for a walk in the fog."

"We haven't had one so magnificent in a long time." Old Man Saburo sounded moved.

No, that's not what I meant. I wasn't talking about gods or whatever, nothing that nebulous. I meant the eerie sounds of the drum and the bell. Something real passed right by us. Was that the god of this mountain? That chilly, unapproachable, quiet presence I felt?

Nobody said another word about it.

"Shall we be off?" said Seiichi, and everyone agreed.

They started down the slope without a care in the world. I had no idea if any of them had heard the sounds or felt that mysterious presence. Creatures on the mountain belong to the mountain, the precinct of the gods. Human beings are intruders and don't stick their noses in what isn't their concern. Kamusari villagers' fearlessness, or should I say their easygoingness, was brought home to me again.

That night, fog still hung lightly over the village, and no fireflies flew over the paddy.

Just about the whole village turned out for Mr. Murata's funeral. His family lived in the center of Shimo district. The river was a bit broader there, and there were more paddies than in Kamusari district. The old Ise Road went across the river. Back in the Tokugawa period, it was thronged with worshippers on their way to and from Ise Shrine, they say. That's hard to imagine today, but the road is lined with several two-story structures like old-time inns.

The Murata residence was set back a ways from the old road. It was a typical farmhouse, with a large front yard, a main house, and a storehouse. Mourners spilled out into the front yard, while inside, a monk dressed in a bright orange robe chanted a sutra. The suit Seiichi lent me was a perfect fit. I offered some incense and then stood in a corner of the yard with Yoki. I had never spoken to Mr. Murata, but seeing his family in tears, I couldn't help feeling sad, too.

To distract myself, I looked around, making observations. Yoki's hair was as blond as ever, even for a funeral. He really stood out. Seiichi and Old Man Saburo were sitting formally in the tatami room. A photograph of Mr. Murata was displayed on the altar. Honest and stubborn to the end—that's how he looked. All around the altar were offerings from the villagers, including a big basket piled high with canned goods, fruit, and all sorts of other stuff, all of it covered with cellophane. Canned goods were not much of a gift in this day and age, it seemed to me, but I figured that must be the custom here.

One thing puzzled me: a tree branch sticking out from the altar, covered in glossy leaves.

"That's star anise," said Yoki. "Traditional at funerals. Also when visiting graves. Don't they use it where you're from?"

I wondered. I'd never seen any before. When our family visited ancestral graves during Bon, in July, we never took a leafy branch with us. We did take flowers.

"It's aromatic and lasts a long time. Around here, star anise is planted in graveyards, and whenever there's a funeral or a memorial service, we cut off a branch."

I barely listened. I had spotted Nao among the mourners standing outside. She was talking to Risa, her eyes slightly downcast.

"Oh, Nao's here. That's right, today's Saturday." Yoki grinned, watching for my reaction.

Meaning what? Today's Saturday so she's able to be here? Almost everybody in Kamusari worked in farming or forestry. They could take time off pretty much whenever they pleased. If Nao couldn't, she must work in the town office or have a company job. At the cherry-blossom-viewing party, she'd said something about a business trip, I remembered.

I made up my mind and asked: "Where does Nao live? I know she's close with Seiichi and Risa."

"Oho." Yoki's grin broadened. "That's what's bothering you?"

"Not especially."

"Now now, don't hide it." He poked me with his elbow. The guy was really annoying. "She lives in Naka district. We went by the shrine on the way here, remember? Near there."

I did remember. It was a fine, big shrine, home to the tutelary god of the clan that settled here back in medieval times, or so I'd heard. The post office and town hall were beside it, so next time I had business there I could look her place up. Or would that make me a stalker?

"Of course she and Risa are close," Yoki said. "Risa's her big sister."

"What?"

The sutra reading had just ended, so my voice rang out over the garden. All eyes turned my way.

Iwao, over by the storehouse, gave me a warning: "Shh!"

Ignoring the attention we were getting, Yoki added casually, "One more thing. She teaches at Kamusari Elementary."

A schoolteacher! The kind of professional that most got under my skin. But having a young, pretty teacher like her would be different. I felt like enrolling in Kamusari Elementary School. Maybe then I'd hit the books.

Now that I knew who Nao was, all that remained was to go over and talk to her. I started off, but Yoki yanked me back.

"Where do you think you're going? It's time to see the coffin off."

"I just wanted to say hi."

"Say hi to who? Never mind. Here, put this on."

I looked at the thing he handed me. *You're kidding me,* I thought. It was a thin white headband with a small triangular piece of cloth attached.

"This is what ghosts wear!"

"Yep."

"How come *I* have to put it on?"

"Not only you. All the men do."

Yoki put on his own headband, wearing the triangle across his forehead, and tied it in back. I looked around. All the men, indoors and out, had on matching ghost headwear.

"This is weird!" I protested. "I could understand if Mr. Murata wore one in his coffin, but why us?"

"Who knows? It's the custom. In the old days, people wore them to the burial, but since everybody gets cremated nowadays, we only wear them when the coffin leaves the house. Hurry up and put it on."

Grown men in black suits were lined up solemnly with white triangles on their foreheads, facing each other. It was freaky as hell. The coffin silently passed between the rows and was loaded into a shiny black car waiting out front. The car horn honked a final farewell.

Mourners who weren't going to the crematorium split up and went home. As I was pushed along in the crowd, my eyes met Nao's. Suddenly embarrassed, I snatched off the white triangular headgear. Kamusari sure had some wacky customs. This one was a bit much for me.

"Ready to go home?" Seiichi said to Risa. "Nao, want to stop by?"

"Maybe I will. I didn't fix anything for supper."

"Stay and eat with us, then," urged Risa.

My heart beat faster. Santa was at Yoki's place with Granny Shige. Since Seiichi and Risa would come by to pick up their son, Nao might come, too.

"Get that dopey smile off your face," said Yoki.

"You're still wearing the cloth," I said.

"So I am." He finally took off the foolish-looking thing.

Just as I'd hoped, Nao came along with the rest of us. What I hadn't expected was her riding her motorcycle wearing a mourning kimono. Holy shit. Riding in the bed of Yoki's truck, I could only marvel as she tucked up her long black skirt and followed behind us. If I stared too hard, she might get the wrong idea. I looked away from her sleek legs and up at the sky. The clouds were breaking up for a change, with patches of blue in between.

Seiichi and Risa thanked Granny Shige for babysitting and left right away with Santa, who was sleepy and cross. *Darn you, Santa. Thanks a lot for wrecking my chance.* I stood and watched wordlessly as Nao pushed her motorcycle and went off with them.

"She won't be easy to win." Yoki folded his arms.

"Don't tease him." Miho patted me on the shoulder. "Yuki, that's the kind of girl you like? A tomboy like Nao?"

Granny Shige giggled.

Darn this whole village. They just can't keep a secret.

Still, it wouldn't do to surrender. The first thing I had to do was somehow talk to Nao.

After supper, I went for a walk to plan my strategy. I eyed Seiichi's house. Maybe she'd already gone home. I didn't have the courage to go and see. Which is ironic, considering my name.

How could I approach her without coming off as a stalker? I started walking toward the rice paddy. Water gurgled in the irrigation ditches. Myriad stars twinkled in the sky. Two more weeks and the rainy season would end. Then the elementary school would let out for summer vacation. After that there was an all-village summer festival, I remembered. Maybe I could invite Nao to that. She might not be interested in younger men, but I could try to get on good terms with her, little by little.

There were more fireflies over the paddy than before. If you'd told me that stars had fallen from the sky and turned into twinkling insects, at that moment I would have believed it. As I looked at the pale winking lights, my heart caught on fire.

As surely as people had birthdays, they each had a deathday, too. Life was short. There was no time to waste. I decided to go to Seiichi's house. My immediate goal was to have a decent conversation. Once I'd decided that, I turned around and started back the way I'd come. In the distance, the sound of a motorcycle engine came closer, along with the light of its headlamp. I jumped out in the middle of the road and waved my arms.

The motorcycle pulled up, and Nao looked at me through her helmet.

"Hi," I said. "Um, I'm Yuki Hirano."

"You already told me that at the cherry-blossom party."

She seemed on the verge of taking off again. Realizing I had to say something, I panicked. Taking things slow wasn't an option. By the time I realized it was a bad idea, the words had already left my mouth: "Please go out with me!"

"Sorry, there's somebody else. See you."

Instant death.

Her red taillight crossed the bridge and receded down the dark mountain road.

I trudged back to Yoki's house.

"Want some tea?" Granny Shige said.

I mumbled an answer, went to my room, and crawled under the covers. Who was this "somebody else"? Was she seeing someone or was that just an excuse to reject me? I'd rushed things. I needed to take more time, let her get to know me. I still didn't know her all that well, either. I wouldn't give up. I'd get back the confidence of "the Yokohama stud." Not that anyone had ever called me that.

One way or another I managed to lift my spirits and face the morning. I had zero interest in going to work that day, but a trainee can't just slack off when he feels like it. Yoki was arguing with Miho over whether he should dye his hair black or not. He sounded like a kid.

I changed into my work clothes, and while I waited for Yoki I went out and looked at the paddy. Where were all those fireflies from last night sleeping now? "Oh!" With a soft cry of excitement, I squatted down. Long, slender rice shoots had shot up, growing in clusters of five. They'd looked like weeds at first, and now here they were, tall and big.

The gods that had descended from the mountaintops in white fog had gently touched the rice, moistening and softening the leaves, and moving the season surely along.

"The department store": that's what everyone called the Nakamuraya, the store Miho's parents ran. The shelves in the narrow, earthen-floor room held everything from food and daily necessities to fertilizer. Santa's favorite toy was a blue water pistol he'd bought there after Granny Shige gave him some spending money and told him to pick out anything he wanted.

There weren't very many young people in the village. Kids of high school age lived with families in town so they could attend the schools there. The only kid below high school age in Kamusari district, believe it or not, was Santa. So naturally, I was appointed to be his playmate. All summer long, I was the target of that water pistol. Water dries off fast enough, so it was no big deal, but my heart really wasn't in it. I would look off at the puffy cumulus clouds beyond the mountains and heave a melancholy sigh. The moment I did, a stream of water would hit me right between the eyes. Santa would giggle and run off.

The days grew hotter and hotter, as if they'd just been waiting for the rainy season to end. The cries of cicadas rained down from the mountains surrounding the village. The air was so clear that rays of sun penetrated my skin and stung. Borne on a warm breeze, the heavy, moist scent of grass filled the house. Rice grew tall, ears of corn swelled on the cornstalks, and fields were full of watermelons. Summer was in full swing.

But in the forestry business, there's no summer vacation. Even in the sweltering heat, the team kept on working. We became soaking wet with sweat. Our work clothes didn't do us much good. The helmet was stuffy, and I couldn't wait to take it off. The tea in our canteens wasn't enough to slake our thirst, so we always had lunch by a mountain stream. We drank water right from the stream and filled our canteens for the afternoon.

No matter how much underbrush we cut, it grew thickly all through the forest. Thinning the forest and carrying loads of brush and timber down the mountain took many times more strength than before.

When you cut underbrush in the summer, you have to watch out for ticks. The ones in the forest aren't like the kind that live in a carpet, either. They're a lot bigger, maybe a quarter of an inch long, so you can see them with the naked eye. Once, when I was working with my sleeves rolled up, I saw one come crawling up my arm. It had a round belly, and I was sure our eyes met. It was so humongous and weird-looking and gross, I let out a yell. "Pipe down, idiot!" Yoki said, and squashed it for me. From then on, no matter how hot it got, I never rolled up my sleeves.

But mountain ticks don't give up easily. They'll crawl in through any gap in your clothes and bite you. And a tick bite itches like crazy. I got bitten on the inside of my thigh. They know right where the skin is the softest.

It happened while I was working. First I felt a kind of prickle. I didn't think anything of it, but pretty soon it started to itch unbearably. The others were working some distance away, and nobody was looking, so I laid down my scythe, pulled down my pants, and looked at my crotch. There it was, a tick clinging to the inside of my thigh. I freaked out a little, crushed it in my fingers, and went back to work, but the itching got steadily worse. It was super-intense, nothing like a mosquito bite. A sensation just short of pain that set my nerves screaming.

After I got back to the house, I examined myself again. The skin was bright red where I'd scratched myself. I sat flat on the tatami, spread my legs, and bent way over to get a good look. I saw two tiny protuberances, like the horns of a stag beetle. What could they be? Then I realized they must be the tick's teeth (do ticks have teeth?). Even while getting crushed, it had never loosened its jaws. Horrified to think the tick's determination and teeth were implanted in my flesh, I let out a yowl.

The *fusuma* door slid open with a bang, and Yoki whacked me on the head. "Pipe down, will you? What is it this time?"

Look! I gestured wordlessly. Yoki got down on his hands and knees and brought his face in for a closer look.

"I'll be damned. You know, you just missed getting bit where it woulda *really* hurt."

What if my cock itched like this, felt this horrible? The mere thought was painful.

Yoki went and got a pair of tweezers and removed the tick teeth with surprising skill, then applied some anti-itch medicine. Since I'd scratched myself hard, it stung like hell. The itch stayed intense for a month.

The trouble with ticks is, there's no way to protect yourself. In summertime, the heat and humidity made the mountains full of danger. But mornings and evenings were cool, and it was cool in the shade, too. I would sit at the foot of a tree on the slope and look up at the blue sky and down at the village enveloped in green until, prompted by the cries of the evening cicadas, I made my way home under wispy orange clouds, thinking from the bottom of my heart how beautiful Kamusari was and how glad I was to be there. But even in the shade of a tree or down by the river, you had to watch out. Dim, damp places had leeches—even grosser than ticks. They sense body heat and creep noiselessly toward you. A tiny gap in a seam of your clothes is enough. Before you know it, one is clamped to your skin, sucking away.

Mountain leeches are tiny, a fraction of an inch long. They're light brown, and they hump along the ground like inchworms or sludge worms. They're so small, and such an undistinguished color, you never know they're there until they've burrowed inside your clothes and are attached to you. It doesn't hurt. Well, sometimes there's a faint prickle— the way rough fibers can rub against your skin and feel a bit scratchy. That's your only clue that something's off.

One day, I felt something funny on my calves, and when we broke for lunch I rolled up my pant legs to see what was going on. Then— ugh, I can hardly stand to remember. Under my right knee there were two leeches, and another three on the left leg. They'd been sucking my blood all morning, so they were swollen ten times their normal size, about two inches long and half an inch across. The color of the blood had turned them black. They were implanted in my flesh as if they'd grown there, wriggling their bodies. The sight was so gruesome I cried out.

I grabbed one in a panic and pulled hard. Looking back, I'm amazed I could bring myself to touch the slimy thing, but I was dead set on getting it off me. The thing was stuck fast and wouldn't budge.

"Not that way," said Iwao. "Pull it off like that, and the head'll stay in."

When a leech is engorged, it falls to the ground and lays eggs. So when you find one sucking blood, you've got to kill it right away. But they're almost impossible to stomp on or rip apart. Their bodies are elastic, and amazingly tough. The only way to kill them is with fire.

Yoki held out the flame of his lighter and torched the leeches. Powerless to resist, they fell off me and shriveled. After the leeches were gone, the bleeding didn't stop. Apparently they inject some kind of anticoagulant into the bloodstream.

"Don't worry," said Old Man Saburo comfortingly. "I never heard tell of anybody bleeding to death from leeches."

Still, I bled so much my pant legs turned bright red from the knee down. Little red circles remained on the skin where each one had attached itself, and for a while they itched.

It wasn't only me, the new guy on the job, who came under attack from ticks and leeches. Even longtime veterans get tick bites and have their blood sucked by leeches. The creatures are a nightmare; no matter how you try to protect yourself, they still come after you. The difference was that Seiichi and the rest didn't fall apart when it happened. "I got myself a tick bite. Itches," they'd say, or "A leech got on me. Hand me your lighter" as casually as they might say, "I'll have another bowl of rice."

Not me. I'll never get used to how gruesome those things are.

My folks called up one time wanting to know what I was going to do for the midsummer Bon holiday. Even if I did get time off, I wasn't planning on going back home. Believe it or not, I didn't want to leave the village for a minute. I didn't want to miss any part of the daily drama of life unfolding all around me with ever-increasing vigor—even if it meant more encounters with ticks and leeches.

That was the power of the summer scene.

In the summer, the village was bursting with life, and there was plenty to do besides forestry work. First off, we had to look after the crops in the field. When we got up in the morning, Yoki, Miho, and I went out to pick vegetables. Every day there were more eggplants and cucumbers and tomatoes, a prodigious amount. We couldn't leave them on the vines, so we picked every last one that was ripe. Corn we picked by twisting the ears from the stalk.

Not just cucumbers but eggplants, too, had sharp thorns on the stem and at the top. I was new to picking them, so I kept yelling, "Ow!" Unlike the produce they sell in the city, in Kamusari even the vegetables are untamed.

Everything we planned on eating ourselves we chilled in a tub filled with well water. The neighbors all had vegetable patches of their own, so sharing wasn't a thing. Every house was overflowing with veggies. What we couldn't eat ourselves, Miho pickled, or Yoki and I loaded it onto the truck and sold it at the co-op supermarket. Our vegetables were irregular and misshapen, but people in town liked them because they were fresh and succulent, with just the right balance of sweetness, bitterness, and acidity.

Corn was Granny Shige's department. She would tear off the leaves (or is it husks? not sure), remove the tassels and strands of silk, and boil the ears in a big pot, or else brush them with soy sauce and cook them over a little hibachi.

All summer long I ate as many cucumbers as a rhinoceros beetle. I ate three ears of corn a day. Half the time Santa would be there, too, munching away on our corn. What we couldn't eat we hung to dry from rafters in the entryway. That way we could go on eating corn all fall and winter, steaming it with rice or soaking it in water to soften it.

When we finished gardening, we went to work on the mountain. In the evening after work, we came back and watered the vegetables. Lots of our neighbors were too old to tend their patches properly, so we'd go around picking their cucumbers and eggplants and tomatoes for them, picking and picking and picking. After that it was finally supper. We'd be bone-tired. And except when I was on the mountain, Santa's water pistol was always trained on me, so I constantly had to be on the alert.

After supper we'd sit on the veranda and have chilled watermelon for dessert. Yoki, Miho, Granny Shige, and I passed a little saltshaker back and forth. We looked up at the stars and spat watermelon seeds onto the ground. For all I know, the seeds flew up into the sky and became stars. It wouldn't surprise me. That's how much watermelon the four of us put away.

Sometimes I ate so much watermelon or corn, I'd get a stomachache. I bet everybody got stomachaches in the summer. But the fresh vegetables and watermelon tasted so good, no one minded.

The trouble was, there was so much work to do, and in between I was so busy eating vegetables and playing with Santa, that there was never any time to sit and think. Think about how I was going to approach Nao, I mean. I hadn't come any closer to finding out more about my rival.

The summer festival is right around the corner. What am I going to do? Just as I was thinking this, Santa would sneak up and score a direct hit on my butt with his water pistol. The village just wouldn't let you sit around and daydream about romance.

Our team was out in front of Seiichi's house one day, polishing wood for use as *tokobashira*, ornamental alcove posts. That's the prominent pillar on one side of a *tokonoma*, the alcove in a traditional Japanese house. Alcove posts are highly decorative features of a room, and often they have interesting gnarls or a wavy pattern on the surface.

"How does wood get to be like this?" I asked Yoki.

All he would say was, "Trade secret."

I found out later that if you fasten disposable chopsticks around the trunk of standing timber, the wood develops a nice wavy pattern as it grows. There's a knack to it, and some people apparently have a special gift. Gnarls form naturally when the trunk gets injured, or some foreign object (an insect, most likely) gets into the wood. The crucial thing, I learned, is judging whether a gnarl is the right shape to make the wood more desirable as a tokobashira. You don't want to go to all the trouble of harvesting wood that just looks defective.

Lately, plenty of people can afford to lavish attention on building a finely crafted house just the way they want it, often with a traditional room that has a tokonoma. Orders for tokobashira are on the rise. The alcove post isn't a mere ornament. It plays a key role in making a tokonoma solid. Timber used for this purpose is left to dry on the slopes for as long as four years. If it's not properly dried, the wood lacks strength and soon splits. Misshapen or twisted wood also lacks strength.

Sometimes a post is made from a log in its natural state, with the bark still on, but the best ones are from what's called side-cut timber, without any pith.

"The core is the center of the tree rings," Iwao told me. "The idea is, you make a post that doesn't include the core, just the rings outside it."

"Then you'd have to start with a log that had a pretty big diameter, wouldn't you?"

"Yep. Like this persimmon here." Iwao pointed to an enormous persimmon log lying on the ground. "Natural wood. It'll fetch a good price, make no mistake." He chuckled.

"By *natural wood* you mean it's not from a tree farm? Then where did it come from? It's huge."

"Trade secret."

There certainly were a lot of secrets.

"Quit gabbing and get to work," Old Man Saburo said. "We've got to polish all of these and get them loaded on the truck before nightfall."

I turned my attention to the task at hand. There in front of Seiichi's house was a big pile of logs that had dried here and there on the slopes of the various mountains around Kamusari (trade secret). They were of all kinds, from camellia logs that would probably be used with the bark on to that persimmon log with the big diameter. Some of them already had the bark stripped off. Our job, which we'd been doing the past several days, was to polish the exposed wood with cloth bags containing fine sand. The friction from the sand brought out a smooth luster and sheen with every stroke.

So beautiful. I gazed in admiration. I was really no help in felling trees or bringing them down the mountain. About the only thing I was decent at was trimming underbrush. But after all, even my mom could pull weeds in our garden at home. So even if I was able to handle myself a little better on the slopes than before, overall I thought my performance was disappointing.

Polishing the posts was different. I could see the results with my own eyes. It gave me a warm sense of accomplishment. Santa kept firing away at me with his water pistol, so the back of my T-shirt was dripping wet not only from sweat, but I paid no attention. *Focus!*

Maybe because I'd pitched in, we were done by a little after three.

Seiichi climbed in the driver's seat of the truck loaded with polished posts. "I'll be back tomorrow evening," he told us, hands on the steering wheel. "Yoki, look after things while I'm gone."

Iwao gave a cheer, and Old Man Saburo shouted, "Good luck!"

The truck, piled with first-class future tokobashira, crossed the bridge and disappeared down the mountain road. At tomorrow's auction, Seiichi would have a chance to display his skills.

The cedars and cypresses that Nakamura Lumber plants are used mainly as construction material. They are the parts behind walls and floors and ceilings, hidden away, unseen. Even if sometimes the wood is used in pillars that can be seen, it lacks the designation "choice wood." Choice wood is natural wood with beautiful grain, color, sheen, and luster that's used for the visible parts of a room. It clearly reflects the builder's taste, aesthetics, and way of thinking. There is no limit to how fussy a buyer can be. Top-quality choice wood often sells for an unbelievable price.

The auction price would affect our pay, too. I offered my own little prayer to the disappearing taillights: *May it sell high.*

A water bullet struck me in the back of the head.

"All right, Santa! I'll get you!" He ran around, but I finally caught him and pinned him down. "Your daddy's not gonna be home tonight. I bet you'll miss him."

"No, I won't!" He laughed and squirmed, trying to get away.

"You sure about that? I heard a monster might come out tonight. If your daddy was here, he'd chase it away, but you'll be all by yourself. What are you going to do?"

"Nothing. Mommy's here."

He tried to sound brave, but he looked like he might cry. Oops, maybe I went a little too far.

With excellent timing, Yoki called, "Santa, want to go to the pool?"

Santa cheered up instantly. "Yeah!"

Pool? Since when was there a swimming pool around here? I was dubious, but Yoki dragged Santa and me to the bridge and then down on the bank. So the "pool" was the Kamusari River?

Yoki waded into the stream, not caring that his pants got wet, and still wearing his jikatabi. He headed straight downstream. Over three hundred feet from the bridge, there was a drop-off of about fifteen feet. A miniature waterfall. Holding Santa in his arms, Yoki looked over the edge at the water below.

"Here we go. Hold your breath."

"Are you kidding me?" My voice, not Santa's, rang out. Before I could stop him, he jumped down, holding on to Santa. They made a huge splash.

"Yoki! Santa!" I waded as close to the drop-off as I dared, leaning over. I was afraid I might lose my footing and be swept away in the tumbling water. Bubbles swirled in the pool below. It seemed as if a long, long time went by.

Finally, Yoki and Santa popped up. Yoki's yellow hair glistened in the sun along with the waterfall spray. Santa waved from Yoki's shoulders. His other hand had a firm grip on the water pistol.

"Go ahead and jump, Yuki!" Yoki called. "Land as close to the waterfall as you can. It's pretty shallow everywhere else."

I couldn't let those two show me up. I worked up my courage and leaped.

Instantly I was in water so cold my heart nearly stopped. The waterfall roared in my ears. The soles of my jikatabi touched a round rock on the riverbed. Damn, it really was shallow. A heck of a place to jump. If you weren't careful, you could hit your head, and you'd be a goner.

I pushed against the riverbed and aimed for the surface. No need to swim; the river was soon shallow enough to stand up in. When I came out of the water into the air, I shivered.

"It's c-c-c-cold."

"You'll get used to it in no time."

Yoki set Santa down in shallow water and set to work piling up stones to make a round enclosure. Of course—a natural outdoor pool. After a while, the water inside, separated from the rushing river, would grow warm in the sun.

"Play here, Santa."

The little boy contentedly stepped over the stones and into the enclosure. He plopped down in the water and proceeded to enjoy himself by alternately filling his water pistol and crawling around like an alligator.

"Hold still a minute, Santa." I crouched down and peered into the pool. When the water quieted, you could see a school of transparent killifish slipping in through gaps between the stones. They swam in apparent wonderment around Santa's soft calves.

"Wow! Look at that. Pretty cool. You've got a pool with fish."

"Wow! Wow!" Santa laughed. For him, seeing fish was no big deal. He had no idea why I was so excited, and with every "Wow" he smacked the water with his palms. The school of killifish scattered instantly, vanishing as completely as if they'd dissolved in the water. I was disappointed, but as long as Santa was having fun, it was all right.

Yoki started rolling boulders, grunting. The guy had superhuman strength, I thought, not for the first time.

"Yuki, gimme a hand here."

I joined him, but all the power came from him. He arranged boulders in a semicircle around the waterfall and pool, filling in the gaps with medium-sized rocks. In no time, the waterfall trickled to a stop. The dam was complete.

"This pool is for grown-ups," Yoki said, and started swimming with his clothes on.

I couldn't wait to join him. I was sweaty from the day's work, and I could just imagine how good it would feel to swim in the cold, clear river water. Eagerly, I jumped from a boulder into the pool. Underwater it was freezing—but exhilarating. With the stream dammed up, the plunge pool was wider and deeper than before. It was probably nine feet to the bottom. The water was transparent, and stones on the riverbed had a blue sheen in the sunlight. A black fish as long as my finger crossed my field of vision. Closer to the drop-off, the water churned, and a jet of fine white bubbles shot up. It was as if there were two waterfalls, one in the air and one underwater.

Unable to hold my breath any longer, reluctantly I surfaced. Immediately my teeth chattered and the racket of cicadas descended with a roar, like a waterfall. I swam the backstroke to warm my belly in the sun. Yoki was swimming like a giant tortoise, with Santa on his back. Both of them had lips so purple, you'd have thought they'd been drinking juice with food coloring. I'm sure my lips were the same color.

Unlike the swimming pool in my high school, here the water temperature was mercilessly cold. The dam couldn't keep the river entirely in check, and the current stole our bodies' warmth as it moved downstream. Still, I wanted to keep playing in the water. I didn't want to get out. Yoki's hand-constructed pool had far greater charm for me than my school swimming pool ever did.

"Hey there!" called a familiar voice. "Looks like fun!" chimed in another.

I glanced up and saw Iwao and Old Man Saburo standing in the road.

"Come on down!" Yoki beckoned to them.

Iwao shook his head. "If I got in there, I'd hurt my back for sure."

"Never mind that. Here you go, Yoki." Old Man Saburo tied a rope around a bamboo basket and lowered it to the surface of the water.

"Got it!" Yoki caught the basket, treading water. In a flash Santa climbed from Yoki's back to his shoulders. He and I peered with great interest into Yoki's bamboo basket. Seen close up, it was a queer shape, like a jar lying on its side. We asked at the same time: "What's this?"

"You don't know?" He sounded so surprised, the blood rushed to my cold cheeks. Santa said, "Nope."

"This is an eel trap. See how it's narrow here." He pointed to the opening. "That's so once the eels get in, they can't get out." He shook the basket with satisfaction. "Caught a whole slew of 'em this time."

Then I realized the trap was full of smooth and glistening eels. "Wow! Where'd all these guys come from?"

"Darned if I know." He sounded put out. "Those two have a secret spot somewhere. I'm pretty sure it's in a branch of this river. One of these days I'll follow them and find out."

"We can never eat all those." After torture by watermelon and corn, were my insides now headed for eel torture? Eels enhance your sex drive, they say. Little good that would do me.

"No, no, no. The summer festival's coming up. Every year our team runs a stall serving char-grilled eel. These are the ingredients."

Yoki got out of the pool and headed for the shallows with Santa still riding on his shoulders. He set the basket in the water and tied it with rope to a tree branch on the bank.

"If we leave 'em here till the day of the festival, they'll be alive and well when the time comes."

"What'll they eat?" The population density of the eel basket was high. I had to ask.

"That's their problem."

"I guess getting themselves trapped in there with no way out is their problem, too."

"All right then, you and Santa are in charge of feeding them," he decreed and went out of the water, shivering. "Brr!"

Yoki decided everything. When we got back, he took over the bath at his place, so I had to use the one at Seiichi's house and be subjected to water pistol attacks while I scrubbed myself.

After a soak in the hot water, I took Santa by the hand, and we went to the department store to buy eel food. Not that they had any such thing for sale, of course. We took the advice of Miho's mother, who was manning the register, and made do with goldfish food instead.

That night Santa wet the bed massively. In the morning, his sheets hung on laundry poles, flapping in the sunshine. Whether it was because he had played in the river, or because I'd scared him by talking about monsters, I couldn't say.

Every day, Iwao and Old Man Saburo would go off somewhere and catch eels, bringing back a trap full of them. Those were transferred to a big bamboo basket, the kind you harvest vegetables in, and left in the river. It was a strange sight, seeing them all lined up. When you looked closely, you could see each basket held a wriggling mass of a dozen or more plump eels with pale green bellies.

I worried someone might make off with a basket, but nobody in Kamusari bothered with crime prevention. The villagers' easygoing spirit prevailed. And the eels stayed right where they were.

Every morning, Santa and I went to check on them and scatter flakes of goldfish food on the baskets.

"You suppose they really eat it?" I would wonder aloud.

Santa would shrug and say, "I dunno."

The alcove posts sold at a good price, so all Nakamura Lumber employees were paid a substantial summer bonus.

Forestry is something of a gamble. When wood sells, it sells like mad, and when it doesn't, it doesn't, no matter how much you knock down the price. You have to wait for just the right time. And while you're waiting, of course, the forests need tending.

It's a sink-or-swim industry, so Yoki and the rest were over the moon when their bonuses came in. The packets arrived a bit later than the customary time for summer bonuses, but no one cared. I even got one, although I was a trainee. The thirty thousand yen in a brown envelope gave me a bit of a thrill. Sure, bonuses were probably bigger at companies in the city, even for new hires. But I was being supplied with everything I needed—food and housing and work. With that in mind, I had to admit that Nakamura Lumber was being awfully generous.

Walking on air, I asked Granny Shige to give me change for one of my bills. I figured I'd need small money when the summer festival came around. I knew that she kept five-hundred-yen coins in the boxes her stomach medicine came in and that she had just started her fifth box.

Before she did anything else, Granny Shige laid my bonus reverently on the Buddhist fish-shaped altar, held her palms together, and mumbled some sort of prayer. She even struck a wooden drum. Then I hoisted her on my back so she could reach around behind the mortuary tablet, where the stomach-medicine boxes were hidden.

"How much do you need?" she asked.

I was only going to buy food at stalls, so I took out a single ten-thousand-yen bill from the envelope.

Granny Shige, sitting on the tatami, opened the box, brought out all the five-hundred-yen coins she had saved, and proceeded to count them off, as if she were playing tiddlywinks.

"There you go, eighteen coins."

I took that in and then said, "How come? You owe me twenty coins, Granny."

"I charge a fee."

Give me a break. I stared unhappily at the eighteen five-hundred-yen coins, and a moment later she started to giggle. "It's a duke," she said.

A duke? Who or what was she talking about? Then it hit me. "You mean a 'joke'?"

She nodded and quietly slid three more coins over.

"Now there's one too many," I said.

"Keep it. You work hard on the mountains, and Granny knows it."

The coins shone silver in the altar room, which was dark even in the daytime. I took the extra coin and wrapped it reverently in my hand. "Thank you, Granny."

She worked her mouth in embarrassment and pretended not to hear.

The sound of a flute rang out sharply in the clear air of a fine day, and I heard a drum, too: the summer festival was getting underway.

People came flocking not just from Kamusari but from other villages nearby. There was a little traffic jam all day, because of all the cars carrying festival participants. The mountain road was barely wider than a path between rice paddies, so that was no surprise.

The festival was held at Old Kamusari Shrine, a different one from the shrine in Naka district. There are tons of shrines all around the village, big and small. Old Kamusari Shrine is on the side of South Mountain. It's got no decoration and is pretty shabby-looking, if you want to know the truth. To get there you have to climb a winding path uphill for about five minutes. Hardly anybody in our district ever goes there, except to take turns sweeping the grounds.

"That's because they're afraid of the god," said Old Man Saburo. "That shrine is the second home of the god who lives on Mt. Kamusari. If people kept going there and disturbing the peace, making a ruckus, it'd make him mad. Best stay away."

"Is it okay to visit the shrine on the day of the festival?" There would be stalls along the whole length of the winding road leading there. Outsiders didn't bother coming this deep into the mountains, so every single stall was run by Kamusari villagers.

"This is the one day it's okay." Old Man Saburo nodded sagely. "The god comes down from the mountain today, and for once he'll grant wishes."

Then maybe I would toss some coins in the shrine's offering box and make a wish. Thoughts of Nao floated through my mind.

Old Man Saburo and I were in front of Seiichi's house. It was just after noon, and already the festival music had started up, but we were still spending all our time getting our stall ready. Everything was spread out on the big table. Preparing the eels for grilling wasn't going well.

"Hyaa!" Yoki, wearing heavy work gloves, would grab a sleek eel from the tub. Bursting with energy, the eel would slip from his grasp and go wriggling off on the gravel. Noko would get excited and strain, eager to go after the eel. It was my job to hold him back.

Yoki would manage to recapture the eel and lay it directly on the table. It seemed to me he could have used a cutting board, but that wasn't his style. The instant the eel was on the table, with a lusty shout Seiichi would swing a huge gimlet to pin it down. The shout was impressive, but half time he missed and only hit the table.

"Whose idea was this division of labor?" Old Man Saburo demanded, waiting impatiently, skewers in hand, for an eel to come his way. Finally he tossed the skewers aside. "We're not getting anywhere this way. Go get Iwao." Iwao had gone on ahead to the shrine to set up our stall.

"It's all right." Seiichi wiped the sweat from his forehead. "I'm getting the hang of it."

Santa reached out gingerly and patted the eel, which was still struggling to escape even though pinned to the table. I knew how Santa felt. He and I had fed and taken care of those eels every day. They were our pets.

Risa and Miho shared a laugh, keeping their distance from our struggles. On festival day, women weren't supposed to do any cooking or other housework. Don't ask me why. That's just the way it had always been, apparently.

I couldn't wait to be off to the festival. It had already started, yet here I was stuck in Seiichi's front yard, carving eels. I heaved a sigh. At this rate, there was no telling when I'd be able to see Nao.

Of course, I was the one Yoki had yelled at for cutting off an eel's head by mistake in the first place: "No, no, you idiot! All right, move aside. From now on, just keep an eye on Noko!"

Our char-grilled eels sold out before the end of the day. The price was cheap, after all: two hundred yen a slice, three hundred for a small bowl with rice (Kamusari's finest). Drawn by the aroma, people clustered around the stall that Iwao had constructed.

Old Man Saburo skewered slices of eel one after another, and Yoki and Iwao grilled them frantically, each with a fan in hand. I slathered the grilled eels with sauce and transferred the finished product to paper plates or bowls of rice. I was so busy that sometimes I got mixed up and instead of scooping rice with my paddle, I started patting an eel with it instead.

Seiichi was in charge of accounts. Of all of us, he alone stayed cool and calm, taking orders with a smile and depositing the receipts in an empty candy box.

"Doesn't seem fair," I griped, wiping beads of sweat from my forehead with the sleeve of my *yukata*. "My right wrist hurts."

"What?" Yoki looked at me with eyes narrowed to slits. He wasn't mad; the smoke and heat hit him straight in the face, and he could hardly open his eyes. "If that's how you feel, tell him you want to change places."

"I can't. *You* get him to trade places with *you*."

"No way." Yoki shook his head firmly. "You know what would happen if Seiichi took over the cooking? The eels would burn to cinders."

So he said, but I knew he was afraid to confront Seiichi. When it came to forestry work, the team members spoke up freely, sometimes voicing their opinions so heatedly you'd have thought they were quarreling. Of course, this was all in Kamusari dialect, so even then they spoke with a slow drawl.

But when it came to anything else, they pretty much did as Seiichi said, every one of them. I understood. It wasn't so much because Seiichi was the master, but more because he emanated a kind of aura or force that was not to be denied. He never scowled or raised his voice. He was mild-mannered and cool. But when he said, "Let's do it this way," everyone fell into line.

He knew full well how to use his powers of persuasion. Today, for example, he had talked his way into the easiest job of all and now sat there smiling like a salesman, smooth and unruffled—while meanwhile, our yukata were soaked with sweat. It wasn't fair.

Our matching yukata, by the way, were brand new, made for the occasion. Granny Shige had sewn them for us. They had indigo stripes, soberly refined and cool. I was wearing a soft *obi* I'd borrowed from Santa, which unfortunately detracted from my soberly refined, cool look.

"This kind of obi is for kids!" I had protested, but Granny Shige scoffed.

"That's not so. Saigo Takamori wore one." She made it sound as if she'd seen him herself, back in the days of the Meiji Restoration.

So I ended up wearing an obi as fluffy as a goldfish tail. Yoki's was gold, like something a singer of *enka* ballads might wear. *Where on earth did he get it?* I wondered.

Yoki had his points, after all. When I said I'd never eaten natural eel, he saved the last serving for me. While Old Man Saburo and Iwao cleaned up and Seiichi counted the money, I stood eating eel from a paper plate. Yoki stood with his hands on his hips and studied my expression expectantly as I chewed.

"Well?"

"It's good."

A faint taste of the sweet, piping-hot meat came through Iwao's special sauce. On Iwao's instructions, the eels' last two days had been spent fasting in a basin of well water. Maybe for that reason, the meat had no strong smell. It tasted as if nothing had ever flowed in the eel's veins but Kamusari's clear, pure water. There was no muddiness, but a rich, deep flavor, like mountain air. The skin was like fragrant tree bark, toasted just right, and the aroma tickled my nose. I had always thought of eel as an indulgence for old men of declining virility, but I was wrong. It tasted fantastically good. With every bite I swallowed, the savory flavor of the fat spread in my mouth, blending perfectly with the *sansho* pepper sprinkled on top. And oh, the sublime texture . . . Was the meat firm because this was a wild freshwater eel, not a farmed one?

"It's really good, but"—I finished chewing—"maybe a little bit tough?"

"Tough?" Yoki seemed worried that something was wrong with his method of preparation. "Lemme see." He grabbed the rest of it off my plate and popped it in his mouth.

"Hey, that's mine!" I reached out frantically, but the rest of my grilled eel—a good half of it—ended up in Yoki's stomach. Dammit.

"The meat's not tough. Your jaws are weak."

Compared to Yoki, who was like a carnivorous dinosaur, everybody's jaws were weak. I watched bitterly as he consumed my eel with apparent satisfaction.

"It's the difference between Kansai and Kanto." Seiichi, having finished his tallying, joined in the conversation. "In Kanto, they steam eel meat before grilling it, but not in Kansai. Here we just grill it as is. That's probably why the texture seemed different to you, Yuki."

"*Steam* it?" Yoki's voice turned a somersault. "You're kidding me. It would turn to mush!"

I hadn't known Kanto eels were steamed, either. An idea struck me. "Seiichi, have you by any chance ever lived somewhere outside of the village?"

Seiichi looked embarrassed. "The difference in cooking methods is common knowledge, I think . . ."

Iwao and Old Man Saburo nodded in agreement.

"I can understand Yuki not knowing," said Iwao. "A young fellow like him. But, Yoki, you should know that much. You're too ignorant."

"He's got cedars on the brain," said Old Man Saburo. "Brain's gone to seed, I mean."

Yoki groaned. "All right, Grampa. Enough with the lame jokes."

Seiichi closed the lid on the box of receipts and turned to me. "Actually," he said, "I did live in Tokyo once. Went to college there. Never could afford to eat eel back then, that's for sure."

"You brought back a wife from there, too, didn't you?" Yoki grinned knowingly.

"What?" I was totally confused. "Wait a minute. Your wife is Risa."

"That's right."

"And Nao is her younger sister, and she lives near the shrine in Naka district."

"Yes."

"Are you saying Risa is from Naka district but you never met her until you both went off to Tokyo?"

"No, no." Old Man Saburo waved a hand. "You've got it wrong. The house by the shrine belonged to Risa and Nao's grandparents. Both of the girls were born and raised in Tokyo."

"We happened to meet in a school club we both joined," Seiichi said. "I talked to her and found out her mother's hometown was Kamusari's Naka district. She used to come here for summer vacation when she was little, until junior high."

"Amazing how you managed to find a girl in Tokyo with connections to this small, underpopulated village," said Yoki. "Talk about lucky in love." He grinned again.

Seiichi brushed off the remark. "It was fate. We naturally grew close. By then her grandparents had already passed and the house in Naka district was standing empty. We fixed it up, and last year after she got her teaching license, Nao moved here, too."

"So Nao lives alone?"

"Yes. We did invite her to live with us." He sounded concerned.

Nao was full of surprises. What was a young woman like her doing moving to a village with nothing but mountains, a place that turned pitch dark when the sun went down?

"When you got married," said Iwao, counting back on his fingers, "Nao was still in junior high. She used to come here on every long vacation. Must've fallen in love with the place."

Yoki grinned insinuatingly for the third time. "With the place or with—who knows?"

Wait . . . Then it hit me. Call it the sixth sense of a guy in love. I stole a look at Seiichi, who was smiling without saying a word.

"Sold out already?" a cheery voice called. Risa emerged from the crowd and headed toward our stall. With her were Miho and Nao, who was holding Santa by the hand. "Oh no, we missed it again this year!"

"If you really want some of our eel, ma'am, you'd better get here early."

Nao looked on from a little distance as Risa and Seiichi talked lightheartedly.

Ah, so my gut feeling was right! But he must be more than ten years older than her. And anyway, he was her sister's husband. *No way. Please, let me be wrong.*

Or maybe this was my chance to come on strong. Really make a play for her: *Forget your forbidden love. There's a better man standing here in front of you.* Nah. I couldn't pull that off in a million years. And unlike Seiichi, I didn't own mountains. But I was a hard worker, even if I was just a trainee. Probably being a trainee wasn't enough. Yeah, but I had great potential. Didn't I?

While I was mulling these things, Santa came scampering up and tugged on my obi. I wished he wouldn't, knowing how easily it could come untied.

"Yu-chan."

"What's up?"

"Buy me some cotton candy."

My first reaction was, *Why me?* But then I looked down at his hopeful face. Oh well. I'd been so busy at the stall I hadn't seen any of the rest of the festival. Why not go for a little stroll?

Santa and I started up the mountain path hand in hand. By then the team had closed up shop and everyone had scattered, melting into the crowd. Risa bowed her head slightly in my direction, in apologetic thanks. No problem. I was used to watching Santa.

Nao was surrounded by a cluster of grade-school kids, probably her pupils, beaming.

The small stone lanterns lining the way up were lit with candles. Stalls hung with incandescent lamps gave off tantalizing smells, mixed with the spirited calls of vendors. There were octopus balls, rice crackers, a shooting gallery, water balloon fishing . . . and the one Santa was making a beeline for, a cotton candy stand. Pink and blue bags of the sweet stuff were on display, printed with cartoon characters. Under a transparent casing, a cloud of spun sugar formed around a wooden chopstick the vendor was wielding. I stared in fascination. Watching someone spin cotton candy always looks like magic.

"Which one do you want?" I asked, pointing to the display, but Santa shook his head. He wasn't interested in the figures on the packages; he wanted to eat the batch he'd just watched being made.

"Those bags have the same stuff inside," I told him.

"No, I want *that*!" he insisted, stubbornly pointing.

Funny kid. When I was his age, I always wanted a bag with a superhero on the front.

The man made Santa an extra-big cloud of cotton candy.

"Smoke, smoke!" Santa exclaimed and happily took a big bite.

"It's made of sugar."

"It's smoke!"

He let me have a bite. The slightly scorched smell and the rough texture, sticky and melting at the same time, were a bit like smoke, I had to admit.

The sound of flutes and drums swelled, along with the buzz and energy of the crowd. A summer breeze blew down from the mountain. My blood stirred. There's just something about a summer festival in the evening.

We finally climbed all the way to the top and went through the old *torii* gate, its red paint peeling. The shrine grounds, too, were packed with people and stalls. Music rained down from a scaffold set up in the center. Bonfires here and there lit up people's smiling faces.

But the forest extending back from the edge of the grounds was dark and impenetrable. Beyond the silhouette of South Mountain rose the peak of Mt. Kamusari. The mountains were silent, unapproachable. No matter how much we humans carried on below them, they never changed.

"Let's go inside." Santa stuck a hand inside the summery blue *jimpei* he was wearing and pulled out a little plastic coin purse. The clasp was too tight for him to open by himself. When I opened it for him, two shiny five-yen coins fell into his hand.

"Mommy gave them to me."

He tried to push one into my hand, but I couldn't take money from a little kid. "That's okay. I'll use my own money."

"No! Oyamazumi-san likes shiny five-yen coins. Have you got any, Yu-chan?"

"No."

"Then use this."

Another village tradition. I took the coin and lined up with Santa in front of the snug little shrine, at the end of the line of worshippers waiting to get in.

The shrine roof was thatched with cedar bark. The building was as old and rundown-looking as the torii. But the festival was lively and crowded, and worshippers were lined up here to pay their respects to the god, so maybe they did get divine help?

"Oyamazumi—is that the name of the god enshrined here?"

"What's *enshrined*?"

"Um, the god who lives here, I mean. Is his name Oyamazumi?"

"Yeah."

I'd heard that name before. The night Santa was spirited away, the villagers had whispered it among themselves.

"What kind of a god is he?"

"Scary." Santa said this in a low voice. "But he watches over us."

Gods were all the same, then. All they did was watch over people. But I guessed that was something to be grateful for.

The line finally moved ahead, and soon we were standing in front of the offering box.

"Yu-chan, what are you going to ask for? Daddy says whatever you ask for on festival night comes true."

Santa pulled on the long bell cord. The bell jangled, and after pondering a moment, I clapped two times and said my prayer: *Make me into a man. One worthy of Nao.* When I opened my eyes, Santa had just finished, too.

"What did you ask for?" I said.

"It's a secret." He covered his mouth with both hands and giggled.

"What! You asked me mine, but yours is a secret?"

Hand in hand, we moved off to make way for the next people in line and left the shrine building.

The sky was now completely dark and filled with winking silver stars. The Kamusari River ran along the foot of South Mountain, shining white in the darkness, while overhead flowed the Milky Way, like the river's reflection.

"Wow," I said. "Isn't the Milky Way gorgeous? You know something? I'd never seen it till I came here."

But Santa wasn't interested in stars. "Let's go scoop goldfish," he said and tugged on my obi again. I really wished he'd cut that out.

He squatted down in front of the goldfish and looked them over, picking out his target.

"Which one you gonna try for?"

"The black one."

"That big pop-eyed one? Forget it. Those are hard to get."

It was a hundred yen a try. Naturally, I paid for Santa's turn as well as my own. I went first, but I had zero luck. A total washout. I never was good at scooping goldfish. I bet if Yoki were there he'd have scooped twenty in a row.

Santa went after his big game, but the thin paper in his scoop soon broke, too.

"Okay, Santa, I'll go again."

"You guys are hopeless!" said a voice full of laughter, right behind us.

The paper in my second scoop broke. *Rats.* I turned around, and sure enough, it was Nao.

"I'll try, too," she said. "One for me," she called to the vendor and handed him a hundred-yen coin. She squatted down between Santa and me. I moved over a little to make room for her, my heart pounding.

"See, the trick is to maneuver the goldfish into a corner . . ." She was completely absorbed. Her profile was really pretty. As I was looking at her, there was a splash, and a red goldfish fell into the little pan she held in one hand.

"Great, Nao!" Santa clapped his hands—and the paper in her scoop broke.

Santa! Thanks a lot! Mentally I scolded him. I could have watched Nao catching goldfish forever.

Nao had her goldfish put into a transparent plastic bag and gave that little laugh of hers. "That's how you do it."

"Well, you only got one," I teased.

"I beg your pardon?"

"And nobody goes away empty-handed, right, mister?"

"Right. Everybody gets one goldfish."

"What about me? I took two turns."

"Doesn't matter. One per customer. But Santa here can have two."

"Thank you."

So all three of us ended up with goldfish. Santa got two, Nao got one (that she rightfully earned), and I got one (as a consolation prize).

She gave another little laugh. "Santa I can see taking home goldfish, but what are you going to do with yours?"

"I thought I'd take it back to Granny Shige for a present." Granny had given me spending money, after all. I swung my bag and looked at the day's gain. The goldfish was tiny. Pale orange. Cute. Granny Shige would probably like it if I put it in a glass bowl and set it in her room.

"Oh, okay," said Nao. "Santa, time for you to go home and go to bed."

"I want to play some more with Yu-chan."

"Well, you can't. Your mother's here." She pointed to a corner of the shrine grounds, where Seiichi and Risa stood beckoning.

"See you tomorrow, Santa. We'll play again after I get home from work."

Reluctantly, Santa nodded. Then he said good night and ran off to join his parents.

I stole a look at Nao beside me. Her eyelashes were waving in the light of the bonfire as she watched Seiichi recede into the distance. The goldfish bag hanging from my fingers weighed heavy.

"Now then," she said, turning to me after Seiichi and his family had disappeared from view. "My sister asked me to pay you back for whatever you spent on Santa. How much is it?"

"It's fine. Forget about it."

The moment I shook my head, my stomach growled. Why oh why did it pick that moment?

So Nao treated me to a plate of fried noodles. We ate standing up, side by side in a corner of the grounds. It tasted really good. In fact, those were the best fried noodles I have ever eaten.

The festival was heating up even more. Over by the music scaffold, Yoki had entered a drinking contest. The participants drank square cupfuls of sake from a barrel offered to the god. There were about five other contestants, including Old Man Saburo. In the end it came down to a duel between him and Yoki. Yoki won on his fourteenth cupful. How could anybody chug that much sake with no ill effects? The guy must have a liver of steel. He was superhuman, no doubt about it.

"I did it!" Yoki cried out in jubilation. "Miho! I'm the *medo*!"

"Stop it, will you? You're embarrassing me." She gave his head a smack.

"What does *medo* mean?" I asked Nao.

She blushed slightly. "I don't really know. You'd better ask Yoki."

"Okay."

Medo medo medo. I said the word over to myself so I wouldn't forget it.

"Are you going to join in?"

"Join in what?"

"Oyamazumi-san—" She broke off. "Never mind. It's nothing. Anyway, you're only here as a trainee."

I felt injured. She wouldn't talk about Oyamazumi-san to me. I'd never be anything but an outsider to her. I wanted to know the story of the god, but most of all I wanted her to acknowledge me, to call me by my name.

121

"My name's Yuki," I reminded her. "And Nao, you're not from here originally, either, are you?"

"No," she admitted. Her face tightened, and she looked straight at me. "But I'm different from you. I've decided to spend the rest of my life here in the village."

I didn't like the tone of her voice, and she still hadn't said my name, and I felt like she was ignoring the hard work I was putting in on the mountains. I was good and annoyed.

"And why is that? Because Seiichi is here?"

How can I describe her face in that instant? If I could go back in time, I'd give myself a swift kick for saying something so idiotic.

She looked surprised, then near tears. Humiliation, embarrassment, and fury showed openly on her face.

"That's none of your business!" she said sharply.

People around us watched in surprise as I stood there dumbly while she stormed off.

Why in the world did I have to say something so hurtful? I was a child. More childish than Santa by far. It wasn't as if I had no experience with girls. I'd had girlfriends. I knew how it was to tell someone you liked her, to hear her say she liked you. I'd broken up with someone and had someone else break up with me. But I'd never done anything as cringeworthy as this. When I was with Nao, I couldn't talk right—not just Kamusari dialect, either. Words wouldn't come.

My shoulders slumped as I watched her walk away. Just as she was about to start down the mountain, she stopped and turned around. I watched, confused, as she came straight back and stopped in front of me.

"Here." She thrust out the little plastic bag with the goldfish, and I took it automatically. "Because just one isn't enough." She turned her back and said over her shoulder. "It's not for you. It's for Granny Shige."

This time, she walked away and didn't come back.

Holding the two bags of goldfish, I murmured, "I love you." Of course, she couldn't hear me. I said the words over and over to myself. *I love you, I love you, Nao. If you'll only forgive me, I'll never be mean to you again.*

I did feel that way, but my brain was full of another thought: *I want her. I want Nao.* I had gone way beyond the level of *There's something about her.* Romance and desire were suddenly linked, my heart and my cock speaking in one voice. *I want you. I want you, Nao. Oh yeah.*

The water in the goldfish bags made little splashing sounds.

I was frustrated. There were hardly any young single women in the village, after all. Nao probably seemed wonderful to me because she was the only one I'd met.

I hadn't intended to go home that summer, but the day after the festival I asked Seiichi for some time off, and he agreed.

Seeing me for the first time in four months, my mom made me fried chicken, pork cutlets, and other favorites. Apparently she decided that for a few days, anyway, she could pay more attention to her son than her grandson.

Sitting around the dinner table with my parents was peaceful. My time in Kamusari must have brought my rebellious phase to an end. I used to think talking to my parents was a drag, but during my visit I found plenty to talk about. I told them about the villagers, about the work, about the leeches. There was no end of stories to tell. Mom laughed and looked worried by turns, and my old man, overshadowed by her as always, just said I looked stronger.

I went down to the shopping area by Yokohama Station to get a battery pack for my phone. The crowds made my head spin, and the amount of goods on the shelves blew me away. Was this really the same country? I'd forgotten how fancy life is in the city.

I walked through the underground arcade in high spirits and bumped into some old friends from high school. My old girlfriend was there, too. Her face was all made up, and her lips were glossy and shining. She really was cute. Nao, I thought, would never wear a camisole.

It was lunchtime, so I joined them for pasta. Back in the village, pasta wasn't an option.

"Whatcha been up to, Yuki? Forestry? Awesome!"

My friends and my ex were all good-natured. We talked about what we had been doing and had a great time. Knowing I wouldn't see them again soon, I was desperately sad when we said goodbye.

But it was no good.

After two days I cut my vacation short and went back to Kamusari. I never did buy that battery pack.

"What happened? Did the mountains call you back?" Yoki laughed.

How much Seiichi sensed I don't know. "The whole time I was in Tokyo, I suffered, too," he said with his usual smile. "On clear days I'd see the Tanzawa Mountains in the distance and think of the mountains here. I'd wonder how a certain section was coming along, when the trees there would be felled."

Only with me, it wasn't the mountains that called me back. It was Nao. Or maybe Nao was like a mountain to me: intimidating and hard to make headway with, but always beautiful.

Granny Shige kept the goldfish. The pair of them swam happily in a goldfish bowl of thin glass that Yoki brought down from the attic. For a while, they lived on the leftovers of the food we'd fed the eels.

Whether Granny Shige gave the goldfish names or not, I don't know. In my mind, I had a special name for the red one, but it's so embarrassing I'll never tell it to anyone as long as I live.

4

THE MOUNTAIN ABLAZE

"This is the greatest view ever!"

Yoki was yelling from atop a camphor tree that must have been a hundred feet tall. I was sitting on a branch below him, enjoying the vastness of the sky and the wind in the trees.

We were on the peak of West Mountain, taking a break from pruning cypresses.

Sometimes, depending on the sunlight and the condition of the soil, cedars and cypresses are planted on the same mountain. Cedars do better where the soil is lean and there's less sun, so generally they're planted below the top, from the eighth station down. (The distance up any mountain is measured in ten stations, with the first at the bottom, the fifth midway up, and the tenth on top.) Cypresses, on the other hand, are planted toward the top of a mountain. They like well-drained soil and plenty of sunshine, and they're more resistant to cold and snow than cedars.

But planting near the top of a mountain means that caring for and harvesting the trees is more work. Just getting to the spot demands a long climb up the face of the mountain. If someone gets injured, you can't get them back quickly to civilization. Deep in the mountains with no one around but each other, Team Nakamura worked cautiously, filled with tension.

There was one inevitable exception—Yoki. The higher the altitude and the greater the risk, the more fired up he got. He especially liked pruning cypresses near the mountaintop. He was so happy, he wouldn't even come down out of the tree at lunchtime. "I'm only going to come back up and prune some more after lunch, so what's the point?" He would tie himself to the tree with a rope and swing like a bagworm, munching his onigiri.

"Best leave him be," said Old Man Saburo. "He's a *hyoitoko*, after all." *Hyoitoko* is a Kamusari word that means "airling"—a creature of the air, someone whose feet scarcely touch the ground.

Noko looked up at Yoki swaying in the tree overhead, then turned to Seiichi and wagged his tail—a sign he wanted water. Seiichi gave him some in a dish woven from bamboo leaves, and he lapped it up. Noko has better table manners than his owner.

Climbing trees is way scarier on a slope than on flat ground. In the beginning, I pruned branches trembling with fear. Cedars and cypresses don't have branches to use as footholds, which is only to be expected since getting rid of them is the whole point of pruning. We also rarely use adjunct ropes to brace ourselves. Attaching and detaching a bunch of ropes all the time would really slow down the work.

Eventually I got used to pruning. The mountain is big, the cypresses innumerable. You have to keep going and just prune. When you lose yourself in the work, there's no room for fear.

After I got acclimated, one day Yoki invited me to climb that camphor tree on our lunch break. The mountains around Kamusari village are planted only with cedars and cypresses, but along the crest, sometimes there's a camphor or other hardwood tree. Foresters will plant one at the edge of a stand of trees as a marker, or leave untouched one that was there to begin with.

On West Mountain, the slope east of the camphor tree belonged to an old man in Naka district. No longer able to look after it himself, he had asked Nakamura Lumber to take over for him. Forest maintenance requires stamina and experience, so folks help each other out. The system is built on generations of trust and cooperation.

The giant camphor tree, with its splendid branches, was perfect for climbing. Also, the bark was strongly aromatic. With leaves tickling my face, I looked down at the frothing sea of green below, and at the village's shining roof-tiles in the distance.

The sky was light blue, not a cloud in sight. The breeze had imperceptibly taken on the crispness of autumn. The idea of swimming in the river had lost its appeal. The trees at the foot of the mountains, down by the village, would soon change colors; persimmons would ripen and turn red.

Animals on the mountains were busy preparing for winter. Sensing their presence, Noko howled at the bushes, his curly white tail wagging hard.

"Okay, Noko, okay!" When Yoki called from the treetop, Noko quieted down a little.

There's definitely something there, though. You sure you want me to ignore it? As if to say as much, he would dig impatiently in the dirt with his front paws. Soon his patience would be exhausted, and he would start howling again.

"He's a hunter, after all." Yoki gave up trying to quiet him and leaned back against the trunk. A hundred feet in the air, he looked as relaxed as if he were chilling on a living room sofa.

I gingerly repositioned myself on my branch. Not looking down is the secret to becoming one with a tree. The minute you become aware of how high in the air you are, your balls shrink with fear.

"Noko stands out in the forest, doesn't he?" I commented. "His coat is really white."

In Kamusari village, nobody shampoos their dog. Once Yoki saw a dog dressed in clothes on TV and cracked up. Noko was pretty unkempt. Compared to the dogs I was used to seeing, I have to say he was grubby-looking. But here on the mountain, he was radiantly, transcendentally white.

"Dogs that are white and smart are worth a lot to forest workers. They stand out at night. If I ever got injured in an accident and couldn't move, Noko's being easy to see would improve my chances of being found."

I was impressed. Who knew such farsighted planning went into the choice of a dog? "But what about wintertime? After a snowfall, Noko would blend right into the scenery."

"Then I'd hug him to stay warm. And if worse came to worst, I could cook me up a batch of dog stew."

Gross. But if worse ever did come to worst, I knew that Yoki would never eat Noko. More likely, he'd cut off his own flesh to feed him. Yoki might not dress Noko up, but no one took better care of their dog than he did. A mountain man and his dog didn't slobber over each other, but they were one in spirit. I always sensed that when I saw the looks that passed between them.

The pruning continued without incident.

I'd made progress, I reflected. I no longer said things like "Seems a shame to cut off a perfectly healthy branch." Pruning is essential to produce knotless timber. Removing unwanted branches helps conserve nutrients, ensures that all the trees get plenty of sunlight, and holds forest fires to a minimum.

Fires happen all the time in timber forests. That's because people who go there to look after the trees build bonfires or smoke cigarettes. A well-pruned forest is fire resistant to some extent, since the trunk is free of lower branches that can catch fire easily. Where pruning is lax and trees have withered branches close to the ground, a wildfire can spread in a flash.

"A forest fire destroys decades of our work," said Iwao. "Stay on your toes to prevent fire and keep the forest in good shape. Don't ever forget, we're only borrowing the land from the god of the mountain."

The cypresses on West Mountain were nearly forty feet high. We were there to prune branches around twenty-five feet off the ground and about two and three-quarters inches in diameter where they joined the tree. We lopped them off, one after another.

You don't just do it blindly. As you may know, branches swell a bit where they connect to the tree. If you cut into the swelling you'd injure the trunk and lower its value as timber. You have to leave the swelling intact and cut at just the right angle, taking into account the shape of the branch and the trunk. Doing this twenty-five or twenty-six feet off the ground, clinging to the trunk, is really nerve-racking. Your arms get tired, and the rope digs into you.

I use a saw. Yoki, of course, uses an ax. Hanging in the air, he swings that ax and chops off the branch unerringly. When he's finished pruning one tree, he throws his rope to the next tree, lassoing it, and jumps. He says it's to save all the energy it would take to climb down and then climb right back up. Again, he seems scarcely human.

"I'm like Tarzan," he says calmly. "Pretty cool, huh?"

If you ask me, he's more like a flying squirrel armed with a deadly weapon—his ax.

Unlike Yoki, when I finished work on a tree, I went down the ladder, positioned it on the next tree, and climbed up again. I used a "centipede ladder," consisting of a plain wooden pole with alternating rungs on either side. I would lean it against the tree and stabilize it by roping it to the trunk in several places.

The days were getting shorter. By five, it was already starting to grow dark. Crows were cawing and the mountains were touched by red, so we called it a day and went home. The evening breeze felt chilly against my skin, while deep inside, the satisfaction of having done a good day's work warmed me to the core. I felt a sense of liberation at being able to go home and eat supper, along with a certain wistful sadness.

"That about does it for West Mountain," said Seiichi as we descended the slope. "It went faster than I expected."

Iwao, carrying the centipede ladder, looked back at me. "We owe that to Yuki."

I was glad and embarrassed at the same time. "That's not true," I said.

"You can say that again," said Yoki, nodding.

Shut up, you. He and I jabbed each other playfully.

Ignoring this, Old Man Saburo asked Seiichi, "What about tomorrow? Are we working in the morning?"

"No, we'll take the morning off."

"What?" Yoki sounded let down. "How come?"

"Have you forgotten? There's a planning meeting tomorrow afternoon about the festival for Oyamazumi-san."

That was the name of the god of Mt. Kamusari, I remembered. "Um . . . the Oyamazumi-san on the mountain?"

Everyone looked at me.

"That reminds me," said Yoki. "What do we do about him?"

Iwao and Old Man Saburo exchanged glances.

Do about me? What's that supposed to mean? My feelings were ruffled.

In answer to my question, Seiichi said, "Yes. Oyamazumi-san lives on Mt. Kamusari. He is the god of Kamusari, and we honor him with a special festival each fall."

The next morning, Seiichi's house was in a fever of preparations for the afternoon meeting. The neighborhood women gathered in the kitchen to help prepare food. Meanwhile, Seiichi greeted villagers as they arrived, Iwao and Old Man Saburo set out cushions and trays, and Yoki . . . had a smoke in the front yard. Except in the mountains, he was of no use at all.

I went back and forth between the kitchen and the sitting room, helping to carry food and drinks. I hoped Nao would be there, but she wasn't. Come to think of it, this was a weekday. A schoolteacher couldn't easily take time off.

Just about every male resident of Shimo, Naka, and Kamusari districts seemed to attend this meeting Seiichi had called. They arrived in pickup trucks, some riding squeezed in the back. Didn't this village have any traffic laws? The pickup trucks spilled out from Seiichi's front yard in a line stretching all the way to the bridge.

With the sliding partitions removed, the main room was enormous, around forty mats big. The sight of so many men of all ages gathered in one room was pretty impressive. The women stayed out of the room. At planning sessions for the autumn festival, henpecked husbands took the lead for once.

When everyone had eaten and had a drink or two, Seiichi broached the subject at hand. "Once again, the day is approaching when we all celebrate Oyamazumi-san. This year will be a grand festival, the first in forty-eight years. Let's all work together to make it a success."

Several grizzled old men got up and talked about what the last grand festival had been like. They spread out an old scroll of some kind and conferred. The group settled on a plan for the day of the festival and proceeded to divide up all the responsibilities among the different districts. I couldn't follow this, so I dozed off in a corner of the room. Yoki lay sprawled on the floor beside me, snoring away.

Three hours after the meeting had started, everything seemed to be more or less settled.

"Finally," said Seiichi, "is there any objection if Yoki takes the role of medo?" He looked around at everyone's faces.

Yoki had been dozing, but at this he jerked awake. "None here!"

Whether they were overpowered by his energetic outburst, or whether they recognized his ability, no one raised any objection. I still didn't know what *medo* meant, but Yoki looked satisfied, so I let it go.

"Master." Mr. Yamane, who was sitting near the middle of the room, spoke up with an air of determination. "What about your trainee? What are you going to do about him?"

"You mean Yuki Hirano. Naturally, I intend to have him participate in the festival."

Murmurs arose around the room.

"I'm afraid . . . I'm afraid I cannot agree to that." Mr. Yamane stammered a little, but his expression was firm. "If an outsider joins the Oyamazumi festival, and a grand festival, too, there's no telling how angry the god may become."

I didn't care about the festival, but Mr. Yamane's attitude ticked me off. He avoided my eyes, as usual. Here I was doing my best to fit in, but whenever I passed him in the street and said hello, he ignored me. I always felt like a ghost or an invisible man. Also, I knew Seiichi and the other team members were getting flak for having hired a greenhorn like me.

Everyone in the room looked hastily from Mr. Yamane to Seiichi and back again. Sometimes they would steal a look at me, too, but quickly avert their eyes. If they had something to say, I wished they'd just say it.

Yoki folded his arms, a cigarette in his mouth, and blew a big stream of smoke from his nostrils. "What is this crap! Quit whispering. All opposed, raise your hand."

No hands went up. That wasn't surprising; Yoki, while telling people to raise their hand, was glaring at every face in the room. I could tell from the atmosphere, though, that plenty of people didn't want me included.

"Very well." Seiichi sighed. "For now we will shelve the issue of whether Yuki participates or not. Please go ahead and make your preparations according to the plan we worked out today."

That night, I was so mad and frustrated I couldn't sleep. I was mad that at his age Mr. Yamane was seriously worried about incurring the anger of the god, and irritated at the villagers, too, for resisting my participation without having the guts to speak out openly. I gave up trying to sleep, threw off the covers, and quietly slid the door open. I felt like talking to someone, but Granny Shige was fast asleep. Even the goldfish were suspended motionless in the bowl by her pillow.

I slipped out into the garden through the glass door in Granny Shige's room. The night was cold and quiet. Noko, asleep in his doghouse, raised his head, but when he saw it was me he buried his chin between his front paws and closed his eyes again.

What were my folks and my friends in Yokohama doing now? If I was never going to be accepted here, maybe I should just turn around and go back. I sat on the veranda and looked up at the dark sky. Before coming to Kamusari village, I'd had no idea that being treated like an outsider could hurt so much.

The sky was spangled with silver. A light covering of gray clouds hid the summit of Mt. Kamusari. From the paddy came the swish of rice plants weighed down by heavy ears of rice. Insects set up a chorus so loud it masked the sound of the river.

Just as I was giving a big yawn, another glass door opened and Yoki came out.

"Whatcha doin'?"

When I didn't answer, he sat down beside me and lit a cigarette. He wore a yukata instead of pajamas, so when he sat cross-legged, his hairy legs showed.

"Go take a peek," he said, pointing to his bedroom.

He insisted, so I put my face up to the glass and looked in. Two futons were laid out in the room. Miho was asleep in one of them. She was lying sprawled facedown, and for some reason her feet were on the pillow. Her covers were on sideways, over her hips.

"Can she breathe?"

"Jever see anything to beat that?" He chuckled. "That's how she sleeps, every night."

I turned back to face the yard. We were silent for a while, absorbing the village's nocturnal sounds and feel. Leaves rustled. Animal eyes shone in the dark. All around, people were deep in dreams.

"You know how when you change schools," said Yoki, "it's hard to fit into the class at first." He stubbed out his cigarette on the veranda.

"I wouldn't know. Never changed schools."

"Same here. You think there's enough schools in this village for people to switch around? I meant in general."

"Right."

"Kamusari is like a school that's gone hundreds of years with no transfer students. So yeah, people say things."

"Right."

"But don't worry. Seiichi's the school principal, and I'm kind of like the school bully, so if anybody gives you a hard time, between the two of us we'll take care of them."

I thought he was joking, but when I looked at him, his profile was serious. I realized he was trying to cheer me up. My mood lightened.

"Yamane's not a bad sort," he said.

"No?"

"What happened is, a couple years ago *he* brought in a trainee. That guy quit his company job and said he was going to devote the rest of his life to forestry, but after just a few months he gave up and took off. That's eating at Yamane. He'd really gone all-out to look out for that guy."

I could understand how Mr. Yamane must feel, but I really wished he wouldn't get me and that other trainee mixed up. What could I do to make him see that I was doing my best to stick it out and fit in, meet the mountains on their own terms?

Somewhere in the distance, the ground made a dull repeating roar like the sound of breakers. *Doh, doh.*

"What's that sound?"

"It's the sound of the mountain. Mt. Kamusari." Yoki got to his feet and murmured with an uncharacteristic scowl, "Could be something's brewing."

Yoki and I weren't the only ones who had heard the sound of the mountain. Seiichi and Iwao both said it woke them up. Old Man Saburo had been in a deep sleep, as well as Granny Shige and Miho.

The next day, the rumbling off the mountain was all anyone could talk about. By way of greeting, people said the mysterious late-night sound was a bad omen, or a good omen, or a mere natural phenomenon and nothing to get worked up about.

A week later, we were out pruning on East Mountain when Yoki said, "Hey, smell that?"

Everyone paused and sniffed the air. It definitely smelled smoky.

Yoki undid the rope around his waist and swiftly mounted the cedar. No sooner had he disappeared among the leaves than we heard him shout, "Fire! The mountain behind the elementary school is on fire!"

Grim-faced, Seiichi shouted back, "Yoki, call the fire department and the town office. Let's all go help put the fire out."

We raced down the mountainside, piled in the pickup truck, and got to Kamusari Elementary as fast as we could. Villagers were congregated on the school grounds, looking anxiously at the mountain behind the school.

White smoke rose high in the air from around the center of the mountain. There was the sudden *crack!* of a tree bursting open, and a cedar was engulfed in flames from the top down. The onlookers murmured.

"This is bad," said Seiichi. "The wind's blowing down from the mountaintop."

"Look sharp," Yoki shouted to the gathering, "or not just the school but the whole village will burn down!" He went to a corner of the grounds and doused himself with water.

I looked on warily. Surely he wasn't going to . . .

"C'mon," he called, "let's stop this fire in its tracks!"

So yeah, he was summoning us to jump into the middle of a forest fire. Um, no thanks. But everyone seemed to take it for granted that we forest workers would do just that. Men from all over the village nodded and shouted encouragement.

The fire brigade came running, dragging a hose. They pumped water from the river and started hosing down the school roof. When the village's lone fire truck arrived, the brigade yielded the school to the firemen and headed up the mountain with the hose across their shoulders. They intended to turn the hose on the forest fire from close up, where the fire truck couldn't reach.

I had no choice but to go along. I made up my mind and doused myself with water to wet my clothes, as Yoki had done.

To contain the fire, the various teams of forest workers were going to cut down trees around the perimeter of the fire. "Our team's been assigned to cut down trees downwind from the fire," Seiichi reported after conferring with men on the other teams.

The students had been evacuated from the building. The teachers, Nao among them, were calmly giving instructions: *Make sure you go straight home. They'll put the fire out in no time, so don't worry, and don't dawdle on the way.*

Watching Nao from the corner of my eye, I plunged into the trees behind the school. As I climbed the slope, rabbits and squirrels fleeing the flames crisscrossed in front of me. Noko howled. The air swayed ominously.

"Might as well start here," said Old Man Saburo.

Seiichi nodded. "We'll work our way upwind as we clear the trees. Stay in a row and call back and forth as you go."

Felling trees is dangerous. Ordinarily, we spread out to minimize the danger, but now speed was of the essence. The sound of chain saws rang out. We worked in pairs. One man made a cut in the trunk while his partner watched to see which way the tree might fall and make sure that all was safe.

"Keh!"

"Hoisa!"

Warning calls and responses echoed across the hillside.

Cedars creaked, then crashed to the ground. Sawing down trees that we had carefully tended was painful, but if we didn't do it, sparks and flames would leap from branch to branch and cause far more damage.

We worked our way up the slope till the air grew so thick with smoke that breathing became a struggle. I went into a coughing fit.

Iwao muttered, "We'll stop here" and switched off his chain saw.

The volunteer fire brigade conducted periodic practice drills in extinguishing forest fires. Now, from the far side of the haze of smoke, members came rushing toward us, hoisting the fire hose.

"Master!" One of them ran up to Seiichi. "We can't do any more."

"What about the helicopter?"

"It should be here in twenty minutes."

"All right. Let's hold on till then."

At Seiichi's order, we retreated downwind, stepping over felled trees. Then, behind a barricade of piled-up trees, we hosed the standing trees.

The crackling flames came closer, splitting and devouring trees as they advanced. Sparks fell from upright, green cedars.

Villagers formed a bucket brigade from the foot of the mountain to the front line of the battle. The pump was working at full power, and several hoses were spraying water continuously, yet still the fire raged and bore down on us. Our efforts had contained the fire, but the flames showed no sign of dying down.

"We're not making any headway." Yoki clucked his tongue.

Iwao, his face black with soot, emptied a bucket of water on the nearby underbrush. Seiichi encouraged the panicky members of the various teams and showed them how to use their hoses to the best advantage. Old Man Saburo, not about to give up, was silently felling trees by himself a short distance away.

Yoki and I were working the same hose. At one point he turned to me and said, "I'm going in closer with the hose."

"What? No! It's too dangerous."

"This way's no good. All we're doing is, whatchacallit, shooting the breeze."

"You mean . . . spitting in the wind?"

"Whatever," he growled. "Anyway, I'm off!" Taking the hose, he stepped across a fallen tree and marched toward the oncoming flames.

"Wait for me!" I didn't like the idea, but how could I let Yoki go alone into that kind of danger?

We crossed over the barricade. A raging hot wind snatched all the moisture from my clothes and hair. Red tongues of flame flickered between the trees, and sparks rained down on the fallen leaves underfoot.

"Hey, you two! Get back here!" Seiichi called frantically, but we didn't look back. Together we supported the hose gushing water. The fat white hose pulsed like an artery. River fish, their bodies shining silver, flew out of the nozzle with the stream.

They'll soon be grilled fish, I thought with detachment.

As the flames leaped and spread, we put out hot spots one by one. Yoki and I didn't speak. Even without words, we knew where to turn the hose next. Besides, in the overpowering heat, opening our mouths would have been impossible. My lips stung. My eyes were half closed; the smoke sent tears coursing down my face.

Then before we knew it, we were standing motionless on the hillside, holding an empty hose. Overhead in the brilliant blue sky of autumn flew a red helicopter, dropping fire retardant.

How come I can see the sky so clearly from here in the forest? Only when that thought went through my mind did my brain register the desolation all around me. The fire had destroyed the forest, leaving blackened cedars standing here and there like charred pillars. On the western slope of the mountain, half the forest had burned to ash, a loss of five hundred cedars. Three and a half hours after it had started, the fire was out.

The fire department later determined the cause of the fire to be a carelessly discarded cigarette. That morning, a group of townsfolk had been gathering mushrooms. People who aren't used to the mountains don't understand the horror of a forest fire and think nothing of tossing aside a cigarette without bothering to stomp it out—never realizing how much time and effort have gone into the care of the trees in the forest.

But no one in the village wanted to point fingers or hunt for the culprit. Fires happen. They approached the disaster philosophically, with their usual calm.

Confronted by the scorched mountainside, everyone fell silent.

We headed home looking like cartoon characters after an explosion— hair on end, faces and clothes smudged black.

When Yoki pulled into the yard, Miho came to the door. He got out of the pickup, took a look at her face, and lowered his eyes. He bit his lip. She came over and quietly embraced him.

I stood to one side, near tears. Granny Shige came hobbling over to me, using a cane. "Thanks for all you did." She gave my butt a pat. I guess she wanted to pat me on the back but couldn't reach that high. I fought back tears, but one trickled down my cheek.

The fire had been terrifying. Watching it destroy trees, I'd felt helpless and frustrated. I wanted to yell and sob, but my pride wouldn't let me.

So Granny Shige can walk when she's got a mind to. I distracted myself with that thought and looked up at the sky, where stars were beginning to appear.

Something was wrong with Noko.

After the fire, he came down the mountain with us, covered in soot, tail drooping. He got in Yoki's pickup truck and went home with us. But ever since, he'd done nothing but lie in front of his doghouse with his head down.

The fire must have traumatized him. Even Yoki and I moped for a few days afterward. Seeing the flames up close had been a shock, and so had losing the cedars. Noko, with no way of knowing what a fire even was, must have been that much more scared. *I got chased by a hot monster!* Is that what he thought?

He stopped eating. Miho, worried about him, bought him some fancy dog food at the supermarket in town, but all he did was sniff at it in his dish and turn away sadly. He would stay inside his doghouse with only his tail sticking out, and when Yoki called him he just gave a perfunctory wag. He stopped coming with us to the mountains—and he used to love roaming in the woods so much.

"I've almost never seen him like this before," said Yoki.

"What do you mean, *almost*?"

"A couple of years ago, I fell on East Mountain."

It happened in a timber forest that had gone untended for dozens of years, in a place Yoki had never been before. The owner had asked Nakamura Lumber to take over maintenance, and Yoki had gone to survey the site, taking just Noko with him.

"The place was full of ferns, the cedar leaves were dense, blocking the sunlight, and it felt like a bear might show up at any moment. I had Noko walk ahead of me, for safety's sake. Then Noko turned around and came back. *Damn,* I thought, *there must be a bear!* I looked all around, but there was no sign of one, and Noko peed on a tree root." Seeing that, Yoki had relaxed and gone on a few steps—and tumbled off a cliff. The ferns had made it hard to see, but there was a sudden ten-foot drop.

"I thought I'd busted my ass," Yoki said. "It hurt like hell. Took me an hour to crawl back up, even though it was only ten feet."

When he finally poked his head over the top of the cliff, Noko came up and wagged his tail apologetically. For the next three months, Yoki said, Noko hardly ate.

"But why? It wasn't his fault you fell down the cliff."

"Don't ask me to explain a dog's conscience."

Yoki said to leave Noko alone and eventually he'd come around, but I couldn't help worrying.

When Seiichi came by to see how Noko was doing, I suggested taking him to a vet. Seiichi grunted and gave a little nod as he looked at Noko. After repeated coaxing, Noko had finally emerged from the doghouse, but he immediately lay down again and wouldn't move. Seiichi and Santa patted him. "What's wrong, Noko?" they said, but his chin stayed on the ground and his ears drooped. He glanced up at Santa for a moment, not moving his head, then abruptly closed his eyes as if he'd lost interest. *Ah, it's the young master come to call, I see. I'm sorry, but please just leave me alone.*

"Is it because the forest fire was so traumatic?" I asked.

"Partly that." Seiichi thought for a moment. "I've got an idea. Help me out."

Yoki was on the veranda, clipping his toenails. Seiichi called him over and explained his plan.

"You really think that'll make him snap out of it?" Yoki was doubtful.

"Definitely worth a try." Seiichi sounded confident.

Firewood was stacked under the eaves in preparation for winter. The earthen-floor kitchen got especially cold, so they heated it with a woodstove. Sticks and logs cut in lengths of eighteen inches or so were piled to about my height.

"The sticks maybe, but not the logs," protested Yoki.

Seiichi was unmoved. "It's all right. They're dried out, so they won't be heavy."

"Yeah, but what if ten or twenty of them fall on me? What if I get hurt?"

"Relax, Yoki," I said. "Don't you care about Noko?"

"Hell yeah, but I care about me, too!"

Ignoring these comments, Seiichi ordered us to our places. He went over to the shadows of the house, and Santa and I followed, leaving Yoki alone in the yard in front of Noko. Noko knew he was there but didn't so much as lift his head.

"Ahem." Yoki gave an artificial cough. "Why, what's this? The firewood looks like it might fall down. Let me see. I'd better restack it."

Peering out from the shadows, Santa and I looked at each other and giggled at Yoki's ham acting.

Yoki crossed in front of Noko and reached toward the stack of firewood. "Uh-oh!" The stack came crashing down—or, to be more precise, Yoki pulled it down. He fell on the ground amid the tumbling avalanche of wood. Noko scrambled to his feet to see what was wrong.

"Help!" Amid the chaos, with several logs on top of him, Yoki called faintly, "I can't move! Save me, Noko!"

The faithful dog rushed to Yoki's side. He nudged an arm with his muzzle, but Yoki didn't get up.

"It's no good. I'm dying." Wriggling like a dying insect, Yoki begged, "Send for help."

Noko seemed unsure what to do. He circled around the fallen Yoki, took Yoki's work pants in his mouth and pulled, licked him on the cheek. Then all of a sudden, like a thunderstorm sweeping in, he sent up an urgent, mournful howl.

Normally, Noko isn't noisy. Even when Santa pulls his ears or grabs his tail, he just lets him. But the moment he realized Yoki was in trouble, he was transformed. Watching him howl in anguish, sounding the alarm, I felt a lump in my throat. Yoki must have been touched, too, because he hastily broke character: "C'mon, Noko! No need to carry on like that."

"That ought to do it," said Seiichi, and he started toward Noko.

All of a sudden the front door burst open and Miho came flying out. "Noko, what on earth—" Then she saw Yoki lying amid the fallen firewood. "Yoki!" she screeched. "What happened?" She raised him up and shook him violently. "Yoki, don't die!"

Well, this was awkward. I looked back at Seiichi. "Um, we forgot to tell Miho what we were doing."

"Yeah. Let's wait a minute and see how it plays out."

With Miho involved, the little show aimed at Noko took on a new level of plausibility. She was shaking Yoki so hard he looked dizzy, as Noko howled encouragement.

"Hold on, Miho. I'm fine. Quit shaking me! My head's spinning." Yoki finally managed to quiet Miho down. Then he turned to Noko and gave him a fierce hug. "Noko, you saved my life! You are the number one dog in all Japan!"

He was still hamming it up, but Noko wagged his tail furiously, delighted to be petted and praised. He sniffed Yoki and, satisfied that he was all right, trotted back to his doghouse as if to say, *Whew. That was a hard job, but I did it.* He went straight to his food dish and proceeded to wolf down the pile of dog food.

Santa clapped his hands. "He's all better!"

"How did he recover so fast?" I said, puzzled.

"You see, Noko felt that he wasn't any help in the forest fire, and he lost confidence," Seiichi explained.

"But a dog can't put out a fire. It wasn't up to him."

"Even so, as a member of the team, his pride was hurt."

Then I understood: by thinking that he'd saved Yoki, Noko had preserved his honor. With his self-confidence restored, he could now get food down his throat. I was amazed to think that even a dog took pride in being part of the team.

Meanwhile Miho was sounding off to Yoki. "What? Are you telling me this was all some kind of charade?"

"Should we say something?" I asked Seiichi.

"No, let's let it go," he said. "Noko's confidence is restored, and Yoki realizes how much he means to Miho. Two birds with one stone."

Sure enough, even as Miho railed at him, Yoki looked fairly pleased.

Santa was racing Noko around the yard.

Sorry we tricked you, Noko. But it's good to see you looking like your old self again.

Seiichi and I picked up the fallen firewood and restacked it. Mt. Kamusari rose majestically over us, touched with crimson at its peak. Red dragonflies flew over the rice paddy, golden ears of rice bowing in the breeze.

Kamusari village, a place where grown men had in all seriousness just put on a show for the sake of a dog. A place that was growing on me more all the time.

Something else changed after the forest fire, not just Noko. The villagers started to look at me a little differently. Most of them had already accepted me, I have to say, but there definitely were some who just didn't take kindly to outsiders. People like Mr. Yamane.

But maybe because I had done my part in putting out the fire, Mr. Yamane's attitude toward me softened. Now when I passed him in the road, he would return my greeting. Well, actually, if I said, "Hello," all he did was nod, but before that he used to totally ignore me. The first time he nodded, I was thrilled. *I did it! I tamed the crabby wild monkey!*

Once during a lunch break in a sunny spot on the mountain, I told that story, and Iwao laughed.

"A monkey, is he! That's pretty rude, Yuki!"

For once Yoki stuck up for me. "It's not his fault Yamane looks like a monkey."

Old Man Saburo had been taking a leak under a nearby tree. He came back, zipping up his trousers. "Yuki did fine work in the fire. That young feller has no call to complain about him."

I was amused to hear Old Man Saburo refer to Mr. Yamane as "that young feller."

Seiichi passed out sausages. "Anyway," he said, "it looks like Yuki will be able to participate in the festival, and that's good."

Excitement was quietly building as the village prepared for the festival honoring Oyamazumi. As usual, I was in the dark, clueless about both the god and the festival. Nearly every day, somewhere in the village, some sort of Shinto ritual was held. If the festival was the presidential election, the little rituals were the primaries. They began and ended before I quite knew it. First I would notice that one or another of the miniature shrines around the village had been swept clean, and then I'd discover shimenawa, those sacred straw ropes, strung across the Kamusari River. People in charge of these preparations seemed intent on doing them unobserved.

"Sweeping the shrines purifies the village from the inside," Iwao explained. "Hanging shimenawa over the river keeps evil from entering the village from the outside. When those things are done, it's time to begin the festival of Oyamazumi-san."

I was surprised by the scale of the effort that went into the preparations. The festival itself took place in mid-November, but the preliminary work went on for more than a month beforehand. As the master, Seiichi was in charge of it all, so he was extra busy.

What surprised me most was when a high wooden scaffold materialized one day in the paddy, just after the rice had been harvested. It was a Saturday in mid-October, so I had the day off, and I went to check it out. A sheaf of rice hung from each corner, and there was a big *taiko* drum on top. Not a soul in sight.

I was mystified, and then early that afternoon, the deep boom of the taiko started up, reverberating through the village. I ran out front to look. A dozen or more men and women were dancing around the tower to the rhythm of the drum. It looked like traditional Bon dancing, but there was no singing. The dancers were silent and expressionless, slowly raising and lowering their arms. And they were all dressed in white. It was eerie.

"It's called the Honen dance." Old Man Saburo was there watching, too. "This means the festival is right around the corner."

"Why don't they sing or clap their hands?"

"Why should they?"

"It looks weird, as if they're communicating with aliens or something."

"The dance is for the god, so of course they've got to be solemn." He spoke with severity.

I still didn't get it. Bon dancing back home was sponsored by the neighborhood association, but they played music over speakers, and it was all a lot livelier. Besides which, they did it literally during the season of Bon, in mid-August. Only a handful of people came to see the Honen dance, and even after the white-robed dancers stopped circling the tower, nobody applauded. What's more, that night the tower was dismantled and removed as if nothing had ever taken place. What was it all about, really?

Anyway, a succession of various ceremonies that I didn't really understand took place, and finally it was time for the festival.

When the day came, after Yoki woke me up early in the morning—to be precise, it was two a.m., the middle of the night—I was made to go through a bunch of rituals. I was strongly tempted to tell the villagers, "You know, I'm cool with being an outsider, after all. I'll just bow out."

Festivals are for eating and drinking and dancing and having fun, right? Not this one. If the summer festival had been the outer face of the village, the Oyamazumi festival was its core identity. The villagers' true nature was laid bare. And by *true nature* I mean at once easygoing and destructive. It was such a hair-raising time, I really started to think

I might die. But before I get into that, I want to write about what happened with Nao.

After the night she gave me the goldfish I'd made zero progress. Not that I'd been sitting around twiddling my thumbs. Nao often dropped in at Seiichi's place, and when I heard her motorcycle go roaring by, I would pop over, too. Yoki teased me, but I didn't care.

Nao and Santa played with coloring books and origami. Sometimes she helped Risa make candied chestnuts. While Santa begged me for piggyback rides, I would steal looks at Nao working in the kitchen. She pretended not to notice and had eyes only for Seiichi. He, however, always maintained a proper distance. His attitude said, *You're my wife's little sister, so you're my little sister, too.* I wondered if he realized how she felt about him. He must. The guy was no dummy. He knew but pretended otherwise. He had no intention of meeting her halfway. I was relieved, but sad for her, too. There she was, right in front of him, and he acted like he couldn't see her. How must she have felt? Just thinking about it made me sad. Her situation was the mirror image of mine.

The unknown factor was Risa. Did she know that her sister was in love with her husband? I watched carefully, but I couldn't tell. Risa was dependable and always cheerful. She showed total trust in Seiichi. I couldn't imagine her going wild with jealousy like Miho, or nursing an unrequited love like Nao, either. Which made her all the harder to read.

"Hell yeah, she knows," said Yoki, grinning. "She stays calm because she's got confidence. She knows she's a damn fine woman and no man of *hers* would ever stray."

Miho pinched him on the thigh. "Well pardon *me* for being the kind of woman that makes my man stray!"

He howled in pain. "I never said that!"

Marital spats always broke out at mealtime. I no longer thought anything of it. Interrupting their sparring, I said, "Yeah, but what about the off chance that something might happen between them? Wouldn't that drive Risa crazy?"

Yoki and Miho both shook their head.

"Impossible," Yoki said. "Seiichi's as upright as a stone statue of Jizo. Fool around with his wife's sister? About as likely as all the mountains of Kamusari going bare. Not happening."

"And Nao is a good kid," said Miho. "She'd never ever do anything to hurt Santa and Risa."

They were right, of course. So all Nao could do was watch over Seiichi and his family and keep her feelings to herself. Must be sheer torment.

Granny Shige had been listening silently, but now she spoke up. "Sometimes a body just has to give up." She took a sip of tea. "Still, there's no guarantee she'd give up and marry *you*, Yuki. That's a different kettle of fish."

"M-marry?" I choked on the word. "I'm not thinking about marriage!"

She giggled. "Never mind. Start by showing her you're a man at the festival."

"Good idea!" Yoki clapped his hands. "Thanks to me, you've got a chance to play a big part in the festival."

"Why *thanks to you*?" I asked.

"I got chosen for medo, remember? The team with the medo plays a central role in the festival. This is your chance to stand out. Perfect."

Medo? I still had no idea what he was talking about. And anyway, in this day and age what kind of woman would fall for somebody who "showed her he was a man at the festival"? I had strong misgivings.

Nao had once quietly said something to me: "That sister of mine really has a nerve." She was busy peeling chestnuts in the kitchen. Only she and I happened to be there at the time. Maybe she was thinking aloud. "You know why Seiichi doesn't use much Kamusari dialect? It's because he doesn't want her to feel lonesome, since she's from Tokyo. Crazy."

I said nothing.

Nao was sitting on a bench on the earthen floor with a bowl of peeled chestnuts in her lap. The blade of the little knife in her hand glinted in the dim interior as she expertly wielded it. Chestnut shells lay scattered on the floor around her feet.

"She's always been that way. Wraps men around her little finger."

The sharp edge in her words seemed to be causing her pain. I had to say something. "You don't hate her, though, do you, Nao?"

"No, I don't. I don't hate her."

She set her hands down for a moment and laughed a little. "I should've been a man. Then I could've joined Seiichi's team like you and worked with him in the forest." She got up to wash the chestnut stain from her hands and sighed. "What a thing to say! Forget I said it, okay?"

How could I? I lingered there in the kitchen until Santa came looking for me, wanting to play.

I'll make you forget him. I couldn't say anything so dramatic, nor did I want to. But I hoped that the coming festival might provide Nao with some kind of release. I decided to do my best to make that happen.

After all, a festival is a time to get excited, go through a near-death experience, and be reborn. Isn't it?

I prepared for the day of the festival with a secret resolve . . . a resolve that kept threatening to weaken and disappear.

The event began with someone blowing a conch shell at two in the morning. The sound reverberated all around the village. At the same time, Yoki threw open the sliding door and came barging into my room.

"Get up! The festival starts now!"

No one told me the festival starts in the middle of the night! I thought in groggy protest as he dragged me from my futon. Granny Shige, waiting in the next room, handed me a bundle wrapped in cloth.

"What's this?"

"Something to change into after the water cleansing ceremony."

W-water cleansing ceremony? I had a really bad feeling about this.

Miho saw us off, striking flint by the doorway. "Come back alive now, you hear me?"

She was a strong woman, but there were signs of tears in her eyes.

"Alive? What's that supposed to mean? C'mon, Miho," I said.

"Don't pay any attention to her. She makes a big deal out of everything." As I wavered in confusion, Yoki pulled me, and we set off for the river. I felt underdressed. Yoki had on a yukata, which he wore instead of pajamas; I was wearing a T-shirt and shorts. The middle of November in Kamusari, I might add, is already winter. Our breath was white in the air. It was freezing cold, and I shivered as we crossed the bridge by the store. The village men were gathered on the other side, several of them holding white lanterns. The light swayed in the gloom of night.

Seiichi began in a solemn voice. "This year's medo is Yoki Iida of Kamusari district. He will be assisted by the Seiichi Nakamura team. The witnesses are the Nisuke Kumotori team of Naka district, and the leaders are the Tsuyoshi Ochiai team of Shimo district. Is there any objection?"

"No," the men all answered together.

What was going on? What was this, some kind of historical play? I stood there openmouthed in amazement as the ceremony continued. The men clapped and began to sing:

> *Serpent na, swim swim*
> *Rabbit na, come come*
> *Kamusari god na,*
> *bring them here.*
> *Naa-naa hoina naa-naa hoina*

As they sang, one after another they went into the river. Yoki was of course the first to take the plunge.

Seriously? It's November, guys. That water is frigging cold.

I stood motionless, but Old Man Saburo and Iwao each grabbed me by an elbow, and in I went, shoes and all.

"*Brr!* It's like ice!"

"Buck up," said Iwao.

"You've got to purify yourself to climb Mt. Kamusari," said Old Man Saburo.

With tears in my eyes I tried to get away, but they wouldn't hear of it. They made me soak in water that was waist-deep.

I thought I was going to have a heart attack. *Cold* doesn't begin to describe the feel of that swirling current. My body hurt, then went numb and lost all sensation. I shook all over with cascading shivers. I was sure every muscle in my body was going to be sore. You know that ad for a diet belt? The one that goes, "It vibrates three thousand times a minute"? Well, believe me, cold water has got to be way more effective than that. I can't guarantee it won't kill you, though.

I stood in the middle of the river, my teeth chattering so hard I couldn't speak. Forming words was impossible. Everything came out "Awa-awa-awa." Meanwhile the "Naa-naa, hoina" chant went on. Men submerged themselves in time to the music or poured cold water over their heads with little wooden buckets they'd brought along.

"Hoina! Hoina!" The one chanting extra loud and throwing water over himself with extra vigor was, naturally, Yoki. I couldn't deal with it.

"Hang on, Yuki," said Iwao. "Just a little bit more."

"Did you feel the water get a little warmer just now?" asked Old Man Saburo. "I peed in it for you."

Eww! Gross! That's disgusting! I wanted to protest vociferously, but all I could do was go, "Awa-awa-awa."

The water purification ritual seemed to last forever, but in actual time it might have been less than five minutes.

"Naa-naa, hoina. Let us hasten to join Oyamazumi-san."

The moment the song ended, the men scrambled up on the river-bank. They stripped out of their wet clothes and dried themselves with white hand towels. Yoki rubbed himself so hard with his towel I thought he might set himself on fire.

In the light of the lanterns, the slight steam our bodies gave off shimmered like heat haze.

The cloth bundle contained a white outfit like those of yamabushi, the ascetic mountain hermits—the same outfit I'd worn when we'd searched for Santa that time he was spirited away. My nose was running, so I sniffed and got dressed. My hands shook so hard, I could hardly fasten the gaiter cords.

"What now?" I asked in a low voice.

"Shh," said Iwao. "No talking till we get to Mt. Kamusari."

The Ochiai team from Shimo district took the lead, staffs in hand. The Kumotori team from Naka district and our team followed behind, single file. Bringing up the rear were men from all the other teams that hadn't been given specific roles to play. Altogether there must have been forty of us. Every man of working age in the village participated.

The procession went along the night road, heading for Mt. Kamusari. By car it would have been a short trip to the foot of the mountain, but walking there took an hour.

Silver stars filled the sky. A cold wind blew down from the mountain, carrying the pleasant scent of fallen leaves. We passed a scattering of houses, dark and silent. We could hear the sounds of the river. Now and then a fish jumped.

After we passed the village cemetery, there were no more houses. The road was pebbly and unpaved. My feet were snug in jikatabi, the same rubber-soled cloth shoes I always wore to work. I stepped firmly on the ground, enjoying the reassuring familiarity of the sensation. By then the shock of the water purification ritual had worn off and the shivering had stopped. The tops of the cedars planted along the road were black, blocking off the sky.

No one said a word. We walked in silence through the night.

Eventually we left the wooded road and the rustling of its trees and arrived at the starting point of the back trail up Mt. Kamusari. A candle was lit in a small shrine. Fresh shimenawa hung between two cedar trees. From this point on, we would climb through dense forest on the narrow, unofficial trail. It must have been past three thirty by then.

The procession halted at a little clearing in front of the shrine. Behind us rushed the abundant waters of the Kamusari River.

Tell me we're not climbing this mountain in the middle of the night!

"Do your best."

A voice sounded in the darkness. Standing in the clearing was a middle-aged guy I'd seen before. Back when I first came to Kamusari, he was the one who put me through basic training. Next to him was a pile of forestry tools. Had he lugged them here all by himself? Could be. I remembered he had the strength to toss a wild boar.

Yoki stepped forward and took an ax. Prompted, I went forward, too—and there was my chain saw! How did it get there?

Everyone on our team picked up a familiar tool. I was getting more and more of a sinking feeling.

Seiichi, as the group representative, faced the shrine and Mt. Kamusari, clapped his hands, and began intoning a solemn prayer:

Humbly we come before you, Oyamazumi, god of Kamusari.
Wairana kateto yasukihio megumitamawanna arigataku chinikome
furifuri yamanisumi boroboro.

What? You don't know what it means? Well, neither did I. This strange incantation that you could hardly record in words went on for about a minute. I *think* he was thanking the god for his protection and blessings, but some of it was gibberish.

He concluded with: "Forever protect the people, the animals, and the trees of the mountains, oh Oyamazumi, and may you remain at peace, naa-naa."

All at once the men shouted, "Hoina!" and I jumped. Seiichi clapped his hands once more. Everyone bowed his head. Old Man Saburo shoved the back of my head, and I, too, bowed to Mt. Kamusari.

Now maybe we can all go home. This faint hope crossed my mind, but of course I was dreaming.

"We're off! Let's give it our all!" Yoki, still holding the ax, began to swing his arms. "Hurry up! Let's not insult the god of Kamusari by letting the sun rise before we get there!"

And with that he charged up the trail.

"Follow him!" Old Man Saburo gave the command, and I joined in pushing forward.

Where were we headed, a battlefield?

The others now broke their silence, whooping and hollering as they climbed. I was left behind in the clearing, faltering, when suddenly a white blur crossed my line of sight. It was Noko. He must have run here all the way from home. Hot on Yoki's scent, he disappeared up the trail.

Dammit. I can't let a dog beat me!

I summoned up my inner resources and set foot on the trail, chain saw in hand.

Why I was climbing Mt. Kamusari, and what might lie ahead when I reached the top, I had no idea.

The forest was deep and dark. In those predawn hours, all that lit up the mountain were the ten or so lanterns carried by the teams charged with being "leaders" and "witnesses." Now and then a winter star shone down through the thick canopy of leaves, but it was no match for the surrounding darkness.

The breathing and body warmth of my fellow climbers kept me going. Now and again I could see Noko running ahead. I focused on him as I followed the pathless path. It seemed we were climbing toward the peak in a nearly perfect straight line.

The slope was steep, and I was panting. My breath hung in the frigid air like white mist. Even Yoki had stopped his war cries. He swung his ax now and then, hacking at vines and brush that blocked the way forward. Noko trotted beside him, his tail wagging as if beckoning to me.

The mountain at night was alive with noises. Birds, their sleep disturbed by our sudden appearance, sounded shrill alarms from the branches of a huge oak tree. Something—a rabbit or a weasel—fled through the bushes, setting branches astir. I sensed that the trees, the birds, and the animals were all watching the movements of the invaders of their territory.

Yet through it all there was a stillness. The wind in the leaves, the animal cries, and the sound of my own breathing were absorbed into the vast stretch of time that had shaped the forest, century upon century.

We climbed for an hour, and although I was sweating, I started to shiver. My body and soul were in tatters. It felt as if they might soon turn to forest fodder. The mountain air so befuddled me that I no longer knew who or where I was, or what I was aiming for.

"Yuki." Seiichi's voice sounded behind me. "Look. Isn't it beautiful?"

I looked where the tip of his chain saw was pointing. It was the stump of a cedar tree, so big a man might just barely get his arms around it. Around the decaying, moss-covered stump, the forest was a little less dense. Next to the stump stood a graceful tree over six feet tall. The slender branches had already shed their leaves and were covered with little red berries that gave off a gentle glow, like city lights seen from afar.

"That's a sandalwood tree," Seiichi said. "See, the mountains aren't only aloof and forbidding. They contain beauty like this. Even with no one around to see, every year the tree bears this fruit."

Seiichi must have been keeping a careful watch over me as I climbed. Thanks to him, I came to myself. I turned, looked back at him, and nodded as if to say, *I'm all right now.*

As though touched by the bright fire of the red sandalwood berries, the sky grew steadily lighter, bluish at first, then tinted the orange of dawn, giving way finally to the pure transparency of morning.

Midway up the slope, I stood stock-still.

The forest on Mt. Kamusari. The place I had been rushing toward in the pitch dark, not even knowing why, was this incredible forest. On the night when Santa was spirited away and we went to search for him, I'd caught glimpses of it. But here, deeper in the mountain, the forest was still more amazing. It was a mass of giant trees: nettle trees easily a hundred feet tall; oak trees, the white undersides of their leaves covering the sky; ancient katsura trees with cracked bark; enormous cedars and cypresses, the likes of which I had never seen on the mountains where we worked. Deciduous trees and evergreens, coniferous trees and hardwoods, all growing jumbled together without the least regard for human-devised categories.

Unlike the mountains covered with timber forests in neat rows, here, in a chaotic order, trees of every variety created a dense tangle of foliage. I thought of the huge persimmon tree I had seen once in Seiichi's yard. It had to have come from here. Finally, I understood.

The forestry business is in decline: people had long been saying this, yet Kamusari village somehow managed to make a go of it. One reason was the systematic and efficient strategy of tree planting and harvesting. Another was the distribution of old and new workers. More than anything, what kept Kamusari going was this mountain. Mt. Kamusari was the object of the villagers' faith, their spiritual sustenance, and the symbol of their pride as mountain dwellers. And it was a precious treasure trove of highly lucrative timber—proof that money does, in fact, grow on trees.

I stood in a daze, looking up at the rich leaf canopy high overhead. I couldn't tell where it began or ended. I kicked a fat tree root with the toe of my jikatabi. I couldn't believe that a forest of such utter magnificence belonged to this tiny village on the island of Honshu.

Did TV stations know about this? If they made a show about Mt. Kamusari, tourists would be sure to flock here. Hey, I might even get a small premium for providing the tip. Instantly ashamed of myself, I banished the thought. *No, no, no.* If their secret forest were revealed to the world, then easygoing or not, the villagers would never let me forget it. They might never let me out—might come after me en masse, brandishing axes. *Yikes.* The thought gave me the shivers.

Why couldn't villagers themselves enter the mountain normally? Why had some of them been reluctant for me to participate in the festival? It was all to protect the mountain. One look at this forest made clear how carefully the villagers had tended the forest through the ages, not felling trees recklessly but tending them carefully to pass on to future generations.

They trusted me and accepted me. I was happy and proud to be there.

The leading Ochiai team shouted that they had made the ridge. Yoki whooped and started running up the slope. Iwao and Old Man Saburo sped up, too, passing me by.

"Let's go. We're almost there now." Encouraged by Seiichi, I started to walk again.

We had ascended straight up the slope from the small shrine at the foot of the mountain, but now the trail looped around. The reason for the detour was soon evident: an enormous boulder blocked the way.

The last part of the climb was the hardest, and I fell back from the rest.

"Hey! What's taking so long?" Yoki was calling from a distance.

With a huge effort, I made it past the boulder and came out on the ridge.

Where was everybody? I looked for a sign of men in white, but the forest was dense and impenetrable. The last thing I wanted to do was get lost. With rising panic, I strained my eyes and ears. Straight ahead, I saw the top of a particularly tall cedar. A red cloth and a white cloth were wafting in the air around it. Were they streamers, festival decorations? I looked closer and saw what clearly looked like two women, one in a red kimono and one in white, their figures floating in midair.

I rubbed my eyes, blinked, and looked up tremulously at the top of the tree again.

No one was there. There was only the majestic green of the cedar against the clear blue of an early winter sky. Naturally. People couldn't possibly fly around the top of a hundred-foot-tall cedar tree. But something told me I would find everyone clustered at the base of that tree. Without hesitation, I walked across the ridge toward the cedar.

Eating on Mt. Kamusari is not allowed. *Why the hell not?* I objected silently. I wanted breakfast. My stomach wouldn't stop growling, so I scooped up some spring water and drank it. Beside me, Noko stared down at the silvery surface of the shining water.

The crowd of men dressed like yamabushi were huddled under that cedar, deep in discussion.

"Come on, Jinsuke, this is no time for joking."

"I'm not joking, Yoki. I'm saying you can do it."

Lots of them were old men, and they were talking fast, so the dialect was harder than usual for me to penetrate. I had no idea what it was all about, but as far as I could tell, Yoki and Jinsuke Kumotori, head of the witnesses, were having a heated debate over something to do with the cedar. Old Man Saburo was egging them on with evident glee, Mr. Yamane was urging them to calm down, and Seiichi was listening silently to both sides of the argument.

Having staved off my hunger with water, I sat down on a big cedar root. Just the part rising from the ground came up as high as my knees. This was the biggest cedar I had ever seen in my life. Its trunk near the roots must be nearly nine feet in diameter. The trunk, rising like a wall, was covered with soft moss. A lizard darted over the moss. On a leafy branch overhead, a bird was singing its heart out. How many creatures called this tree home? I leaned my temple against the trunk, and the bark felt cool and moist on my skin.

"This tree is a thousand years old if it's a day." Iwao separated from the circle of arguing men and sat down next to me. "Not hollow, either. It's a beauty."

"Can you tell by looking if a tree is hollow or not?"

"Generally, yes. You can tell by the spread of the branches and the condition of the leaves."

I nodded, impressed, and then closed my eyes and leaned back against the trunk.

A wind swept through the mountain, and from somewhere came the sound of falling leaves.

"I saw the strangest thing before," I said. "Two women were flying around the top of this tree. I was lost, and they saved me."

I expected him to laugh and tell me I'd been dreaming, but he said calmly, "Is that so? One in a red kimono and one in white, was that it?"

"Yes. Made of some beautiful, thin material."

"Those are the daughters of Oyamazumi-san." He patted me on the shoulder. "Good for you, Yuki. The god of the mountain likes you."

Iwao was dead serious. The solemnity of the forest must have gotten to me, because I ended up thinking maybe he was right; maybe such things really did happen.

Suddenly Yoki raised his ax high. "All right, if you insist, I, Yoki Iida, will do it!"

The men shouted in approval and clapped.

"What's all that about?" I looked dispassionately at the group.

Iwao got to his feet with a grunt. "They've settled on a plan for cutting down the tree."

"What! They're going to cut down this tree?"

They were going to do just that. It seemed that at the grand festival, they cut down one of the giant trees of the forest.

"The rest of the time," explained Seiichi, "we cut down a younger tree, barely one or two hundred years old. Last year it was a persimmon."

Even a "young" tree was a century or more old. I worried that one day they might cut down all the trees in the forest, but apparently there was no fear of that.

"We always plant a sapling of the same kind in the same place. Even without our tending to it, in the end some kind of tree will grow." Seiichi looked up fondly at the gigantic cedar. "The tradition of cutting trees on Mt. Kamusari goes far back in time. No one knows when it began."

"Isn't it forbidden now to cut down trees a thousand years old?" I asked.

"Our village has special permission to cut one down every forty-eight years. It's an important ritual."

"What do you do with the tree after you cut it down?"

"You want to know?" Seiichi chuckled. "You'll soon find out."

I had an uneasy feeling and prayed silently: *Please let me get off the mountain safely, in one piece.*

Our team, led by Seiichi, would do the main work of felling the tree. Yoki set to work doing preparatory bending and stretching while Iwao explained the plan to me.

"See here." He spread out a map of the mountain and pointed to a spot on the ridge. "This is where we are. The thousand-year-old tree is standing almost vertical, just below the top of the ridge."

"Okay."

"We're going to cut it so it falls west at an angle of fifteen degrees."

Cutting down a tree at right angles to the crest is nearly impossible. And to the west of the thousand-year-old cedar stood miscellaneous trees about fifty feet tall, blocking the area where the cedar was to hit the ground.

"Why west, when there are all those trees in the way?" I asked.

"Look over there. See the chute?"

Iwao was pointing east of the cedar. A timber chute had been designed crosswise along the slope of the mountain. The Kumotori team had spent two weeks building it, he said.

I remembered hearing about the huge chutes used to slide timber, built like rafts out of oak and cedar logs. Sudden realization hit me. I gulped. "Are we going to send the old cedar down the chute?" I asked. "All of it?"

"Yep." He chuckled as if it were no big deal. "The trunk's heavier toward the bottom, so it goes down bottom first. That's why the tree has to be felled so the top points west."

"Does the chute go all the way down to the foot of the mountain?"

"No. We came around a big boulder on the way up, remember? The chute only goes that far. From there on, the trail leads straight down, so that's all you need."

Then from the boulder on, the gigantic cedar would race to the bottom at high speed.

Nooo! I don't want any part of a project so terrifying!

I screamed this in my mind, in perfect Kamusari dialect.

Without the slightest regard for my preferences, preparations continued. Seiichi took sake someone had brought and poured it all around the foot of the tree. We faced the tree and solemnly clapped our hands in unison. *If we're going to treat the tree with such reverence, wouldn't it be better not to cut it down?*

Everyone put on a helmet and goggles to protect against flying sawdust and chips. These clashed with our old-fashioned yamabushi getups, I thought, tempted to laugh out loud, but the others remained solemn.

Yoki walked around the cedar, taking its measure from every direction, like a golfer reading the green before making his putt. Finally he staked out a spot. "Here!" He tapped the trunk twice with his ax handle, then lifted the ax high in the air and held it poised, ready to swing.

The men began to chant:

> *Hoina hoina*
> *Oyamazumi-san*
> *Look upon us now*
> *as with utmost skill we hew*
> *the cedar you have granted*
> *Hoina hoina*

Kan! With a dry, ringing sound, the ax blade made the first incision. The bark split, revealing the fresh whiteness of the wood beneath and releasing the fragrant cedar aroma.

Yoki began by chopping a notch on the west, creating an undercut. If he got the angle and direction wrong, the tree wouldn't fall as intended. This step was crucial to the success of the undertaking. The village secret, passed along from generation to generation, was to make the undercut as if you were carving out a triangular block.

Next, from the opposite side of the tree, he would make the felling cut. The undercut and the felling cut are like the entrance and exit of a tunnel. Chopping down a tree is a lot like digging a tunnel from both ends—but the tunnel must *not* go all the way through. Around the midpoint, you have to leave a hinge. Without that crucial hinge, the tree will teeter and crash in some unpredictable direction. If the felling cut is done properly, then the tree falls slowly toward the undercut, with the hinge as fulcrum. At least that's how it works with ordinary trees. This time, Yoki was up against a greater challenge than even he had ever faced. At its thickest, I'd say the thousand-year-old tree was over thirty feet around.

After wielding his ax with superhuman prowess, Yoki stopped to sharpen it. While he was busy doing that, the rest of the team crowded around and used a chain saw to make the felling cut. We took turns, working closely in sync and making sure to keep the bottom of the notch level.

The buzz of the chain saw echoed over Mt. Kamusari like the sound of a warped guitar. Birds flew off in surprise. A huge amount of sawdust sprayed out and piled around our feet. The spire of the tree swayed as if in agony.

"Yoki," said Seiichi, setting down his chain saw, "it's nearly ready."

"All right!" Yoki stood before the tree again, his freshly sharpened ax in hand. "I'll aim for the acorn trees" (by which he meant konara oaks).

If a tree as ancient and enormous as the cedar fell flat against the ground, its own weight, plus the shock, might cause the trunk to break or split. Yoki had announced his intention to cushion the cedar's fall with the thicket to the west. Of course, for the konara oaks, being used as a cushion was an unmitigated disaster, equivalent to a bicycle cart getting slammed by a dump truck. Any cushioning trees would be crushed to smithereens.

"Rest in peace, acorn trees! Squirrels, I'm sorry to take your food! Forgive me!"

After apologizing to the squirrels for robbing them of their acorns, Yoki got into position, ax raised. He was a blue-white flame of determination. The other men all hightailed it, heading up to the mountain crest to avoid being trapped under the tree. Team Nakamura had complete confidence in Yoki's skill. We knew the tree was going to fall exactly where he said it would, and so the four of us stayed put, right behind him.

Yoki's ax rang out again and again, deepening the felling notch. Finally the grand old tree began slanting west. The tip descended in a wide arc. The konara oaks were crushed to bits. Time seemed to slow down.

At the violence of the impact, the ground thrust upward, bringing me to my senses. The ancient cedar lay where it had thudded to rest. The exposed tree rings on the cut surface (it's called a "transverse section") gleamed momentarily white in the forest before contact with the air turned them light brown.

The thunder of the crash echoed back and forth among the mountains encircling Kamusari village for what seemed a very long time.

"That was something, Yoki," Old Man Saburo said with deep emotion. "Never seen a tree felled so neat and clean."

The other men came rushing forward, dancing and singing, "Hoina hoina." As they mobbed him, Yoki looked at us with a proud smile. Seiichi and Iwao nodded in return.

I'm ashamed to admit it, but somehow my vision clouded over with tears. All I could think was, *Oh wow.* My legs shook.

If Yoki had been born in the city and grown up with no knowledge of forestry, what might have become of him? Wherever he was born, he would have lived life fearlessly and with gusto, I had no doubt of that. But he would've turned into the guy who chases women all the time and goofs off when the boss isn't looking. That our brilliant Yoki, blessed with the ability, the aptitude, and the instincts of a top forester, should have been born in Kamusari with a deep love of the mountains seemed nothing short of miraculous.

Yoki was loved by the god of Kamusari. That was all I could think after watching him fell the thousand-year-old cedar with a grace and power that verged on mystical. He seemed transfigured, shining with divine light.

It was past noon, and my hunger, too, had fallen away. We'd been on the move constantly since two a.m., but the exaltation of the festival fueled us. Nobody complained of being sleepy or tired.

Thanks to Yoki, the thousand-year-old cedar was aimed straight at the chute. We would be able to lift it into position with minimal effort. First we trimmed all the branches, each one the size of an ordinary cedar. All forty of us worked together till we were dripping with sweat. We were done in an hour—testimony to the amazing toughness of the local men.

Shorn of its branches, the thousand-year-old cedar was now a log. The bark was left on. The log was so huge that the more I stared at it, the stranger I felt, as if I'd wandered into a world where things were out of scale.

"Even if it gets to the foot of the mountain, what earthly use is a giant log like this?" I muttered, seated on top of it. The top of the log was so high that I'd had to use a centipede ladder to climb up.

Yoki climbed up, too, a reluctant Noko in his arms. "No worries," he said, having apparently overheard me thinking out loud. "A tree used in the grand festival is lucky, so orders come in from all over."

I gave him a doubtful look. "Before I came here, I'd never heard of the village or the festival, either one. Orders from where?"

Noko was acting scared, so Yoki set him in his lap. "Don't be snotty. Believe me, people are eager to have a giant tree that was felled for a Shinto festival. They take the whole thing. Last year's cypress went to a gang in Osaka."

"Yakuza? Really?"

"They're superstitious. They'd been renovating the boss's house, so they forked over a pretty penny."

"How much do you think this one will go for?"

"Ask Seiichi. He's the registered owner of Mt. Kamusari." Yoki rubbed his thumb over the tips of his index and middle fingers with a knowing smile. "It's worth a bundle, that's for sure. A shrine in Hokuriku has already staked a claim."

I marveled at the existence of a world I had never known. My folks' place in Yokohama was ready-built housing basically made of plywood.

Seiichi called, "Come on, up there! Quit goofing around and get to work!"

"Yes, sir!" answered Yoki. To me he griped, "Sheesh! He sounds like a schoolteacher."

He put Noko back on the ground and then, his actions belying his words, set feverishly to work. The thousand-year-old cedar had to be off the mountain before sunset.

Some ten feet up from the transverse section, Yoki chiseled a pair of holes and filled them with stout oak poles about as big around as a two-liter soft drink bottle. They stuck out from the log like horns on a cow or a dragon.

Yoki grasped one of the poles and said in satisfaction, "There's the medo. Being able to set up the medo is the greatest honor there is for a woodsman."

They were just ordinary poles, as far as I could see. Then Yoki whipped out a knife and began adeptly carving them, adding indentations or grooves. He did them both the same way.

What was this, some kind of decoration? As I watched, I felt my face turn red. "Yoki, don't tell me these are . . ."

"Peckers!" He threw out his chest with pride. "The medo are pecker symbols."

What? Why go to all the trouble of felling a thousand-year-old cedar and then jam pecker-shaped poles in it? When Yoki was chosen as medo at the summer festival, Miho had looked embarrassed. Now I knew why.

In confusion I blurted, "If that's what a medo is, all you need is one!" It came out in Yokohama dialect.

"That's true, now that you mention it," Yoki agreed. "Maybe long ago people figured having two would be twice as much fun."

I gave up.

While Yoki worked cheerfully on his creations, Old Man Saburo and Iwao trimmed the transverse section, smoothing and shaping it. You know the wooden beams they use to strike temple bells, how they're kind of worn and rounded at the end? It was like that.

"This way, going down the mountain the wood doesn't get damaged," Iwao explained.

"If there was a crash, this would soften the impact," said Old Man Saburo.

Crash? I felt another wave of uneasiness.

Straw ropes were fastened securely to the medo. The ropes ran along the full length of the cedar trunk, fastened in place here and there with wooden stakes. If the thousand-year-old cedar was a dragon, the medo were its horns and the ropes were reins.

What were the straw ropes for? Why were they fastened into place like lifelines? My uneasiness was mounting. I started having palpitations.

Jinsuke had been watching our team at work, and now he stood on the thousand-year-old cedar stump and announced, "It's almost time. Everyone, let's join forces and pull!"

"Hoina!" came the response.

The forty of us, each holding a stout stick, gathered around the gigantic log. Using our sticks as levers, we lifted the log slightly in the air and quickly slid narrow logs beneath it. ("Narrow" only in comparison to the thousand-year-old cedar, of course.) Then, using the ropes, we rolled the log forward. They say that's how the Egyptian pyramids got built, too—by rolling huge stones over logs. It was like that.

Finally it was in place, so precariously balanced that it seemed at any moment it might start to slip down the slope on the chute. Straw ropes fastened the medo on the front of the ancient cedar to cypress trees on either side. It was as if the giant cedar was champing at the bit, eager to take on the giant slide, barely restrained by the ropes.

"All right, everybody on!" Yoki shouted the order.

He was standing toward the front of the log, grasping a medo. I didn't think it was a pretty picture. But if you didn't know the medo were penis shaped, you'd think he was bravely riding the back of a dragon, holding on to its horn.

What did he mean by *everybody on*? The men were all rushing to climb up on the cedar log and hold tight to one of the straw ropes running down its back. Their faces were full of determination not to be shaken loose.

I'm sure I turned pale. *Don't tell me we're getting up on this log about to take a header down the slope? Ride along as it careens through dense forest all the way to the foot of the mountain? No way! No frigging way!*

The log was not just gigantic but round, like any log, and therefore unstable. The way down would be full of obstacles—trees and rocks and god knew what. With no way to steer, how were we supposed to make it to the bottom in one piece?

My team was in place at the head of the log, all of them holding fast to a medo. One by one they called down to me.

"What are you waiting for, Yuki?" yelled Iwao. "Come on up!"

"Hurry, before the sun goes down," urged Old Man Saburo.

"Thanks to me, you get to hold on to a medo." This from Yoki.

Seiichi added encouragement. "This experience is incredibly auspicious and lucky. Much more than the one at Naritasan Shrine where sumo wrestlers throw roasted soybeans and people try to catch them in their mouth." I'd never actually done that, but I'd seen it on TV. Happens every year on the day before the beginning of spring on the lunar calendar.

After coming this far, it wouldn't do to hold up the festival. Timorously I got back up on the log and grabbed the left-hand medo, standing alongside Seiichi and Yoki. Iwao and Old Man Saburo were holding the one on the right.

"I bet people have died in this festival," I said, feeling desperate.

"Eight, according to ancient records." Old Man Saburo tossed this tidbit off as if it were nothing.

Eight recorded deaths. Great. I'd be number nine. I was confident in my unluckiness.

"Don't worry," said Seiichi. "You may be a trainee, but you're registered with Nakamura Lumber, so you're entitled to workman's compensation."

That wasn't really what was weighing on my mind, but thanks.

"Are you shaking? What a chicken!" Yoki laughed uproariously.

Fine. You're not afraid. I get it. You haven't got a sensitive bone in your body. I railed at him silently and turned for support to Iwao, who struck me as the most sensible member of the team.

"You're afraid, too, aren't you, Iwao?"

"Not for a minute." He beamed. "I was spirited away, don't forget. The god of Kamusari likes me, so he's not going to let anything happen to me during his festival, now, is he?" He was maddeningly confident.

"Listen, everyone." Seiichi solemnly addressed the group. "Are you ready, men?"

They answered in one voice: "Yes!"

Not me! I'm not ready!

"All right then, we're off!"

With an ax, Seiichi cut the ropes tying the log to the cypresses on either side. Just then Noko came charging toward us, baying, and leaped from the cedar stump to land by my feet. Meanwhile, with the deliberation of a roller coaster at the top of a hill, the cedar log slowly moved forward, its nose tipping down. We each had a covered chain saw tied on our back, and for one second I felt mine lift up and hang in the air.

Aaghhh! I screamed in silence as the ancient log began to slide down the slope.

"Hoina!" The men whooped and hollered, hanging on for dear life. The ropes creaked. With a dry popping sound, chute logs broke under the colossal weight of the giant log. Splinters and wood chips struck my goggles. Branches projecting over the course battered my cheeks, and I yelled in pain.

"Watch out, or you'll bite your tongue!" Yoki said.

On we catapulted. It felt like riding on an old steam locomotive—a runaway train that kept rushing ahead even as ties broke and the track fell apart under its wheels. The reckless, coal-shoveling engineer was, of course, Yoki. On this ride wilder than any roller coaster imaginable, he stood swaying, gripping the medo, laughing and shouting, "Go, go!" I couldn't believe him. Seiichi was even more unbelievable: he stood calm and erect at the head of the speeding log, his expression serene as always.

These guys weren't human.

Old Man Saburo let out little puffs of breath, hanging tight to the medo. I couldn't tell if he was scared or excited. Iwao was muttering something under his breath. I listened closely, and it sounded like a prayer for protection.

Instead of praying you'll live through it, better to abolish this ritual and stop courting death!

Shouts and screams came from the men behind us:

"Agh, it's swaying!"

"We're done for!"

"Mommy!"

Their voices held a note of laughter and a kind of exaltation. When excitement passes a certain point, it seems that restraints are cast to the wind and a welter of emotions rises to the surface.

Looking back now, I can be analytical, but trust me, while that thousand-year-old log was going hell-bent down the slope, coherent thought was impossible. I was afraid I might piss myself. My hands were clammy with sweat. It was all I could do to hang on to the medo.

Fallen leaves covering the ground were churned to whirling dust. Birds panicked. Through deciduous branches as narrow as cracks, I watched them flee skyward, calling frantically to one another.

Scenery rushed past in the blink of an eye. The giant cedar log might be the shape of a dragon, but its way of rushing forward was more like a wild boar. The beauty of the forest was reduced to an incoherent blur of colors and shapes, as if a bucketful of green, brown, and red paint had been flung sideways against my vision.

The angle of descent steepened, and we went still faster. My sleeves ballooned in the wind.

Noko yelped sadly. At my feet, he had dug his claws into the cedar bark, bracing himself to the full, but his strength gave out. A slight sideways roll of the log sent him up into the air. Out of the corner of my eye I saw his fluffy tail go slowly by.

"Noko!"

Instantly I reached out with my left arm and grabbed him around the hindquarters as he was blowing away. My body twisted; I couldn't support my weight with just one hand. My right hand slipped away from the medo.

I'm going to die!

In that moment, everything happened in vivid slow motion.

Two rows of men clinging to straw ropes gaped up at me as I started to dive, still holding Noko. Mr. Yamane mouthed the word *No!* Noko's tail shrunk and went between his legs. My left hand strengthened its grip on him, burrowing into his fur. I wasn't letting go, no matter what. If I let go, Noko would die, and I couldn't let that happen.

Behind the onrushing cedar log, a pair of women hovered in the air. I couldn't make out their faces. I could only see that they wore kimonos, one red and the other white. The daughters of Oyamazumi. Were they here for me? Was I going to crash into the ground with Noko and die? I contemplated the questions with strange detachment.

The two women gracefully raised their arms and pointed behind me.

At that very moment I heard Yoki call my name. Still clutching Noko, I looked back. Yoki was holding on to the medo with his left hand and extending an ax handle toward me with his right. Seiichi, one arm clamped around Yoki to steady him, was regarding me with, for once, a look of extreme anxiety.

"Grab hold!" Yoki yelled.

I grabbed. Stretching out my right arm, I latched onto the well-worn, smooth-as-silk wooden handle. I felt myself being drawn with immense power toward the medo, toward where Yoki and Seiichi stood, toward life and away from death.

A vein bulged at Yoki's temple. "C'mon c'mon c'mon!" he bellowed.

Putting every ounce of strength I had into my right arm, I bellowed back: "Coming!"

I pitched forward and found myself standing once again between Yoki and Seiichi. Swiftly I grasped the medo.

It had felt like an excruciatingly long time, but it must all have happened in a flash. Behind me, the men let out shouts of relief and joy.

I'm alive. The moment I realized that, I started dripping sweat. Droplets from my face were swept back by the wind onto the men behind. *Sorry, guys. Didn't mean to rain sweat on you.*

"You idiot!" Yoki was panting. "You could have died!"

But I'd needed to save Noko. What I'd done was reckless, I knew, but I had no regrets. Pressed close to me, his ears flat against his head, Noko was shivering as he looked up at me in abject apology. I was glad. Both of us were alive. And warm.

Wait a minute. For real, my middle feels warm. Aagh!

I moved the arm holding Noko and looked down. "Noko, you peed on me!" My white robe had a yellow stain.

"Ah." Yoki nodded. "Happy pee, eh, Noko?"

I didn't think so. I thought he'd wet himself in terror.

"Anyway," said Seiichi, "I'm glad you're all right." He patted me on the back.

172

I turned cautiously and looked back. Nowhere among the rapidly receding trees was there any sign of the two women. They might have been an illusion, but in my heart I said a prayer of gratitude. *Thanks for saving me.*

"Thanks for saving him." Yoki said this with perfect timing, as if reading my mind. I looked at him in astonishment, but he of course was thanking me, not the daughters of Oyamazumi-san. He patted Noko's head awkwardly.

I laid Noko carefully by my feet, once my breathing and pulse settled down—although since the log was still racing downhill at breakneck speed, my heartbeat was way faster than usual. I gripped Noko between my legs to keep him from getting blown away again.

"Out of the frying pan and into the fire," said Old Man Saburo.

"Ready or not, here it comes!" yelled Iwao.

The big boulder, where the chute ended, was fast approaching. To get on the mountain trail we'd climbed early that morning, we needed to make a sharp right turn.

"How do you get this thing to change direction?" I shouted, but no one answered. Yoki, Seiichi, Iwao, and Old Man Saburo stood braced against the medo, their faces grim. The men behind us, who until a moment ago had been letting out sporadic cheers of *Hoina hoina,* were silent. The only sound was the rushing of wind in my ears.

Tension streaked like lightning through the thousand-year-old cedar log.

Surely . . . I swallowed hard. *Surely we're not going to crash into that boulder?*

"Noooo!" I shrieked. "We'll all die! Let me off!"

"This is it," said Seiichi.

"Hang on!" cried Yoki.

Instinctively we all bent over and tucked in our heads. I was pressing Noko tightly between my legs and he yelped in pain, but I couldn't help it.

A shock that felt violent enough to rip my insides apart tore through me. The cedar log struck the boulder, its left half mounting on top of it, and rebounded. Like a runaway horse rearing up with its forelegs pawing the air, the log went almost vertical.

"Ahhh!" Pulled by gravity, my feet slipped out from under me. I hung from the medo, my entire weight (plus Noko's) supported by my arms.

The cedar log began a slow tilt to the right, mowing down trees as it turned. Hitting the boulder had enabled us to change direction.

The giant cedar fell in a wide arc, twisting, toward the trail. I braced myself against the crushing power of centrifugal force and clung fast to the medo.

We landed on the trail with an earth-shaking thud. I clenched my teeth to keep from biting my tongue. All of a sudden my nose ran. My goggles were wet with tears and sweat. Now if excess momentum caused the cedar to roll over or break, every one of us was a goner. *Please, just slide nicely on down the trail!* I prayed, hunched over, as the thousand-year-old cedar bounced twice, three times, bounding and skipping along.

Something flew overhead, just skimming me. Caught by surprise, I looked up and followed the unknown flying object with my eyes.

It was Mr. Yamane. He must have lost his grip on the straw rope. He whizzed past, flailing in midair.

Instinctively I started up, but jumping off to rescue him was out of the question. The cedar log had just settled firmly on the trail and was starting its final descent toward the foot of the mountain.

"Yamane!"

"You okay?"

Shouts arose from the men behind us. With the log now stabilized, everyone turned and looked back at Mr. Yamane as he flew off. He followed a gently curving trajectory and landed on his back in the crown of a cedar alongside the trail. Leaving behind the swaying branches of the cedar and Mr. Yamane, who was no doubt impaled there, the thousand-year-old cedar went steamrolling ahead.

"Do something!" I yelled at Yoki and Seiichi, standing beside me by the medo. "Mr. Yamane . . ."

Seiichi frowned. "I'd like to, but what can I do?"

He had a point. We were barreling forward, unable to stop. We couldn't go back for Mr. Yamane. Still, it seemed heartless.

As I started to lash out, Yoki said easily, "Relax. From the look of it, he's not dead. Those branches cushioned his fall."

All I could do was hope he was right.

After starting down the trail, the thousand-year-old cedar was picking up even more speed. The men behind us raised their voices in woe. Whether they were concerned more about Mr. Yamane or their own safety aboard the hurtling juggernaut, who could say?

Ahead of us was a faint light. The trees were more spread out. The far-off sounds of flute and drum grew louder all the time. In response, the men took up the chant again: "Hoina hoina."

The foot of Mt. Kamusari was close at hand.

But wait. Making it safely there was one thing. How would they get this hurtling projectile to stop? At the entrance to Mt. Kamusari was the little stone shrine and the clearing, that's all. Beyond that was a valley dug out by the Kamusari River.

What the—! If this thing doesn't stop in the clearing, we'll go head over heels into the river!

My hair stood on end.

"Hoina hoina."

As the men chanted, women below responded in chorus, their voices light and inviting, as if to soothe the raging cedar log.

"Hoina hoina."

It was like passing straight through a curtain of green. Finally the thousand-year-old cedar reached the bottom of the slope and slid on into the clearing. The stone shrine was crushed flat. Pieces of scraped tree bark flew in the air.

The dragon lifted its head high, and I squinted at the sudden brightness of the unhindered sunshine. It was dazzling. I never knew the winter sun could be so powerful. For the first time I sensed just how dark and deep the forest had been.

Even after coming out on level ground, the cedar did not lose momentum. On it plowed over the gravel, raising a shower of small stones.

Just about the entire village had turned out to greet the arrival of the thousand-year-old cedar. Most of them were women, including Miho, Granny Shige, who was sitting on a rush mat, Risa, and Nao. There were also old men who had retired from forestry. They all cheered when the cedar log came out with us aboard, laughing as they fled to safety before its headlong dash.

Everyone scattered. Since Granny Shige couldn't run, Miho shielded her with her body. Risa and Nao stood beside them, looking up at us as we grasped the medo.

I must have taken in the entire scene in an instant.

"Stop!" I yelled at the charging cedar. Everyone else was yelling, too—Yoki, Seiichi, Old Man Saburo, Iwao, and all the rest.

Invisible brakes must have heard our command. The thousand-year-old cedar came to rest, jutting one quarter over the Kamusari River cliffside.

A momentary silence was broken by jubilant shouts of "Hoina!" I let my goggles hang around my neck, raised both fists in the air, and gave a wordless whoop of exhilaration. A number of helmets were flung into the air.

The villagers in the clearing clapped their hands and jumped for joy as they gathered around. Noko crawled unsteadily away and made straight for Miho's arms. The men behind us all got off the log, either by using a centipede ladder or by impatiently sliding down the side, and stood around congratulating each other on the successful completion of the rite.

Yoki and I did a high five, and Iwao and I shook hands. Old Man Saburo swung his arms to loosen his shoulders, murmuring, "Well, well." Seiichi removed his helmet and bowed deeply toward Mt. Kamusari.

And so the grand festival held just once every forty-eight years, the ritual of bringing a giant tree down from Mt. Kamusari, came safely to an end.

What happened to Mr. Yamane, you say? He survived. Not only did he survive, but after dark he came down from the mountain under his own power! The cedar branches had cushioned his fall, just as Yoki had said they would. He got off with just a bit of bruising. We were so glad to see him, we held a drinking party around the thousand-year-old cedar in his honor. Although actually, the party started before he ever got there. In fact, we were so far gone by the time he arrived, we'd almost forgotten he was missing. What if he'd been stuck somewhere on the mountain, unable to move all that time? I hate to think.

But this was easygoing Kamusari village, after all. Even if he'd died, they probably would have taken it right in stride: *So be it. That's just the way it goes.* Sometimes they could be so laid back, they seemed downright coldhearted. I guess they took it for granted that you entered the mountains at your own peril.

Right after he came panting into the clearing, Mr. Yamane downed three glasses of cold sake and laughed. "What a time I had!" Everyone crowded around to commiserate and offer congratulations: "You surely did!" "Thank goodness you're all right!" And so on. And that was that.

The party went on all night.

The white moon rose over the mountain rim and gently lit up the mossy bark on the thousand-year-old cedar. We warmed ourselves at bonfires while feasting on food in picnic boxes and dancing whenever someone started to play the flute. It was so cold you could see your breath, but beneath the strung-up paper lanterns, every face was smiling.

Santa was lying with his head in Risa's lap, covered with a jacket. As the evening wore on, he had become exhausted. Noko was snuggled up to him for warmth, curled into a ball with his eyes shut.

The village women showed no sign of winding down. While we were climbing Mt. Kamusari, cutting down the cedar tree, and then speeding down the mountain at the risk of our lives, they had packed food and brought it to the clearing along with bottles of sake. While waiting for the giant tree to appear, they had prepared the lanterns and bonfires and drunk sake to the festive music of drum and flute. They'd been in the clearing, drinking, since noon. But even late into the night, they showed no signs of inebriation and carried on with gusto, drinking and laughing boisterously.

Empty sake bottles lay scattered on the ground. There was even a barrel of sake. This amount of drinking wasn't normal. Maybe the villagers were really *bakemono*, monsters in disguise. Just as this suspicion rose in my mind, Yoki called my name. I turned, and there in a corner of the clearing, seated in a circle on rush matting, was everyone in our team but Seiichi. Granny Shige, Miho, and Nao were there, too.

"Hurry up, come on over," said Miho, beckoning to me. Her cheeks were slightly flushed from the sake.

Nao didn't seem to mind my presence, either. *Let her be a bakemono. I don't care. She's so beautiful.* Granny Shige, on the other hand, was a wrinkled bean-jam-bun bakemono. Thinking this, I grinned, but tried not to show it as I joined the little party.

"This was your first-ever festival, but you did us proud," said Iwao as he filled my cup with green tea, before I had time to tell him I was drinking orange juice. Iwao was already pretty drunk.

"Waiting was fun, too," said Miho with a smile. "As the old cedar came down the mountain, it kept startling birds and making them take off in flight. So we always knew exactly where you were."

"When the cedar landed, I couldn't help myself. I worshiped it." Granny Shige demonstrated by placing her palms together. "Nobody got hurt, and that's wonderful."

"I bet you weren't the only one who felt worshipful." Old Man Saburo said this in a strangely loud voice. "All the women who saw Yuki holding the medo must have fallen in love with him." As he spoke, he gave Nao little glances.

Ah, so that's it. I was grateful they were trying to get us together, but their method lacked subtlety. Feeling awkward, I looked casually around the clearing. No sign of Seiichi.

Miho whispered in my ear, "If you're looking for the master, he took Risa and Santa home."

"Don't let this chance go by, Yuki," said Granny Shige encouragingly. Because she's half deaf, she didn't lower her voice.

What to do? I was in a pickle. Even with them openly smoothing the way for me, there was no guarantee Nao would like it. She must have known what everyone in the circle was thinking, but she gave no outward sign—never even looked at me—but just tipped her cup up and took a sip.

This did not look at all promising. Unable to speak, I drank my green tea–orange juice blend. It tasted awful.

Yoki, sitting cross-legged, jiggled his knees in frustration. "All right," he said, "Yuki, I yield the right of medo to you."

Whoa. Old Man Saburo and Iwao cried out in surprise. Granny Shige snickered, and Miho looked at Yoki as if she wanted to say something. The only ones who weren't sure what was going on were Nao and me, the village newcomers. But I had a disturbing premonition.

"Um," I said tentatively, "so what exactly would that be?"

"The man who brings down the tree from the mountain in the grand festival is the medo." Yoki puffed out his chest and said boldly, "He's got the right to ask any woman he likes to sleep with him!"

I hadn't had anything alcoholic to drink, but I felt dizzy. I put a hand on the matting to steady myself. This was way more than I had bargained for.

"Just who were you planning to use the right of medo with?" Miho asked Yoki, dead serious.

"Don't be silly. You, of course." He put his arm around her shoulder. "That's why I'm saying I'll give it to Yuki. I don't have to ask you, I just always . . ."

"Stop it! You're embarrassing me."

"Nothing to be embarrassed about. Don't be shy, now."

Yoki and Miho started carrying on as if they might go off into the bushes any minute. Crazy couple!

As I blushed over the unbelievable right that had been ceded to me, Old Man Saburo poked me. "Go on, Yuki."

Easy for him to say. I looked up at Nao. She was red-faced, too. When our eyes met, she looked away. Her profile, embraced by the lantern light, shone white in the darkness, more beautiful even than in any of my dreams.

"Nao."

"No."

"I didn't say anything yet."

"You don't have to. I know what's coming."

Dammit. She could at least let me get the words out. I plunged on.

"Nao, I really like you. Please go on a date with me!"

"A date?" she said in a small voice. "Where?"

Good point. Where could we go? There weren't any suitable places for dating in the village.

"S-somewhere in the woods?" I stammered, knowing it sounded more like a picnic than a date.

But Nao gave a faint nod. "Okay. No harm in a date."

Iwao and Old Man Saburo had been watching breathlessly. At her answer, they clapped and shouted their approval.

"I'll pack you a lunch," said Miho. Her lunches were always the same: jumbo onigiri, no frills.

"Now if you two have young'uns," said Granny Shige, "that'll help stop the village depopulation." She was getting *way* ahead of herself.

"This is too tame," complained Yoki. "I gave you the right of medo! What about *that*?"

"I'll hang on to it, for sure." Against the day when Nao might like me back.

"Suit yourself, but don't get any ideas," said Nao. "Not a chance you'll ever use it. It's pointless."

Her coldness gave me a thrill. Still does. Does that make me a masochist? No, I've learned not to give up. Growing trees takes years and years. You can't succeed in forestry unless you have a temperament unperturbed by the elements, however harsh the wind and snow.

I looked up at the night sky, light of heart. After its blazing colors in the heat of the autumn festival, Mt. Kamusari had regained its normal quiet. Its crest overlaid with glittering stars, the mountain kept watch over the village and the villagers.

5

TAKING IT EASY IN KAMUSARI

My long record of the past year in Kamusari village is coming to an end. Thanks, everyone, for reading it! Not that I've shown the contents of this computer to a living soul. This is my secret record. But when I tell myself that *maybe* someone is reading it, the sentences come a lot easier.

Wait a minute. Yoki couldn't be reading it on the sly, could he? I hope not. I'd hate for him to find out all my embarrassing inner thoughts.

I just went to the family room to check on things. Yoki and Granny Shige were munching rice crackers while they watched TV. They don't seem to realize that I've been busy writing lately. Anyway, Yoki doesn't know his way around a computer. Whew.

In between tapping the keyboard, I took a look at my hands, and I realized how thick and callused my palms have become. These days, handling the chain saw on the mountain doesn't bother me in the least. It hurt like hell when my blisters popped, but now it's like I have a whole new set of hands. This is the first time in my life I ever worked so hard on something that it physically changed me. Maybe if I'd studied hard enough in high school to get calluses from writing, I wouldn't have been sent here in the first place.

But I have no regrets. I'm glad I got to live in Kamusari. Before the snow came, I went on a few dates with Nao in the mountains. Picnics, I should say. We'd wear jackets and gloves (mine were heavy work gloves) and walk on the hillside. The tree bark was hard, just before winter, but we saw deer munching away. Thick layers of fallen leaves made the ground soft. On bare tree branches, birds whose names I don't know would fluff their feathers to keep warm.

We sat under a big oak tree and ate Miho's jumbo onigiri. We drank the pure water of the mountain stream. The sky was a clear light blue, and Kamusari village was wrapped in the thin pale light of winter. We didn't talk much, but I had a great time. I think Nao, sitting next to me, did, too. Her vibe of *Keep away, don't talk to me* has gradually weakened.

We're not exactly dating, but for two acquaintances in the same village, we sure spend a lot of time together. She's not just a good friend, either. It's a hard-to-pin-down kind of relationship.

If this were the city, with tons of other people around, I think I'd probably be telling myself she's too much trouble, that it's time to move on. But here in Kamusari, it's like Granny Shige says: "You've come this far. You're almost there. There's nobody around to compete with, so don't rush. If a boy and a girl spend time together, they'll naturally get sweet on each other."

I don't think it's that simple, but she's right about there being no competition. Or no eligible competition. I'm well aware that Nao still follows Seiichi around with her eyes. I think I'll just let things ride for now, and wait.

But I'm not sitting by with my arms folded. I'm putting a plan into motion to show off my good qualities. I buckle down to work every day, determined to make myself into an ace forester. First I'll do some pruning and help carry out dry timber, and after the snow piles up, I'll help with snow removal and lay straw over the roots of cedar saplings in the field. There's a lot to do.

It seems as if we do the same things over and over as the seasons change, but that's not really true. That's what I've come to understand over the course of this year. The mountains are different every single day. Moment by moment, a tree grows or withers. The changes may be subtle, but if you miss those subtle signs, you can't grow healthy trees and you can't maintain the woodlands in optimum condition. I learned this from watching Yoki, Seiichi, Old Man Saburo, and Iwao at work.

It gives me great pleasure to find small changes on the mountain. Just as much pleasure as realizing that lately, Nao has been smiling at me more.

Today is February 7. A day when it's forbidden to go into the mountains here. From old times, lots of people have been severely injured on this date, so eventually they made it a rule that no forest work is done on February 7.

Instead, everybody in the village gets invited to Seiichi's place in the evening for dinner and sake. I went over this morning to help with the preparations. The women of the village were out in full force in the kitchen, boiling and frying and making festive dishes like *chirashizushi*—sushi rice topped with sashimi, egg, cucumber, and other good stuff. Nao was there, too, so I was planning to watch for a chance to talk to her while slicing lotus root in a corner . . . but Miho soon chased me away.

"Go on, leave us alone, will you? We womenfolk have a lot of things to talk over among ourselves. Just go on home."

The women in the kitchen giggled at me. They all know I'm stuck on Nao, so it was kind of awkward.

I wasn't the only one shut out of the kitchen. Seiichi was in the living room, watching TV with Santa.

"It's the women who run things in this village, you know," he said. "All we can do is wait around till the party starts." He sounded bored. When there's no forest work to do, the master loses all authority.

So I spent the afternoon typing this, and Yoki and Granny Shige are watching TV. I'll bet every television in the village is on right now. And the ones watching are all men with nothing better to do.

I wish time would hurry. I can't wait for the party. There'll be good things to eat, and I'll see Nao.

I know: I'll write about New Year's. Vacation ends here on January 2, so I didn't go back home for the holiday. It was the first time in my life I didn't spend New Year's with my folks, so I thought I'd miss them, but I was wrong. I thought they might miss me, but I was wrong there, too. They went to Hawaii for New Year's. Acting like celebrities or something.

After the holiday, a package came for me. It was chocolate-covered macadamia nuts. Whatever. Why do people who go to Hawaii always buy those? There must be other Hawaiian souvenirs. A letter came with the package. "Your father and I are on our second honeymoon! Yuki, work hard and do your best. Give our regards to everyone."

They seem fine. That's nice. Yoki scarfed all the chocolate.

Where was I? Oh yeah, New Year's.

Our team got together for New Year's Eve at Seiichi's house. Nao was there, too. Santa insisted he'd stay up till midnight, but he fell asleep even before the second half of the NHK singing competition on TV. Way too early.

"Santa always goes to bed at eight and gets up at five thirty," Risa explained. I was blown away by how healthy that sounded. He's just a little kid of course.

Something else blew me away. I always assumed Iwao was single, but it turned out he's got a wife. She works in the forestry co-op, apparently. I'd seen her around, but I never dreamed she was married to him. She told me, "Our son wasn't interested in forestry, so he went off to Osaka. My husband was thrilled to have you come, Yuki."

Around the time the temple bell began tolling the old year out, there was a noise out in the front yard. Over at Yoki's place, Noko was howling like crazy. I looked out front, and under the big wood-plank table I saw the gleam of an animal's eyes.

"There's something out there," I said.

Yoki came over. "Lemme see, lemme see," he said tipsily and peered out. "Tanuki—racoon dog. Ground's covered in snow and poor thing's hungry."

"Perfect timing," said Miho. "I just finished frying some tempura to go with the New Year's noodles. Let's give him a little."

"No!" shouted Old Man Saburo.

"Why not?"

"About twenty years ago, we gave tempura to a tanuki. It poisoned him, and he fell over dead."

"Eh?" I looked dubious, so Old Man Saburo appealed to Granny Shige.

"That's what happened, isn't it?"

"Yes, it surely is." She nodded. "Butterbur scape tempura. Made it myself."

"This is shrimp and vegetables." Miho held out the platter for us to see.

"Doesn't matter what was in the tempura," said Yoki. "I'll bet the tanuki went belly up because it was Granny Shige who made it."

"What's that supposed to mean!" Granny Shige gave him a swat on the head.

"Anyway, you mustn't do it!" Old Man Saburo insisted. "Tempura kills tanuki!"

Nobody felt like tempting fate, so Risa put out some tangerines and boiled eggs.

Santa said that in the morning, the food had disappeared. There were tiny tracks in the snow and a spray of red camellias on the doorstep. Not a thank-you from the tanuki but Yoki's mischief, I'll bet.

Old Man Saburo was a widower and lived alone, so he spent New Year's Day with Seiichi and his family. Yoki, Granny Shige, Nao, and

I ate New Year's *zoni* soup flavored with miso, and visited the little shrine at the foot of Mt. Kamusari. After being destroyed by the thousand-year-old cedar, it had been rebuilt at the end of the year. Every forty-eight years when the grand festival rolls around, the shrine gets wrecked. The villagers anticipate that and have a special reserve fund to pay for the reconstruction.

January 2 is *kirizome*, "first cutting," the first day of work in the new year. It's not full-scale work, though. People go into the mountains and dig up a handy small tree. The snow is deep, but they don't go very far into the mountain, so it's pretty easy. The trees they dig up are distributed around the neighborhood and displayed in every yard, branches attached.

I wondered about this, so I asked Iwao. "Um, what's the tree in the yard for?"

"What's it for? Well . . . Tell him, Old Man Saburo."

"Eh?" Old Man Saburo was sprinkling refined sake on the tree and helping himself to some while he was at it. "Nothing special that I know of."

"It's like a Christmas tree, or the bamboo branch for the star festival, isn't it?" Yoki, who'd been playing with Noko, brushed off his knees and stood up. "Except it's on its side."

Seiichi looked down at the tree lying on its side in his yard and said, "Decorate it with paper strips like we do for the star festival, then."

Iwao summed it up. "Why, I don't know, but it's traditional."

There are a lot of traditions no one really understands in Kamusari village. I had to accept Iwao's explanation.

Yoki actually did put colored paper strips on the tree in our front yard, with New Year's resolutions on them: "Fell ten thousand trees." "No hangovers (as much as possible)." Santa was looking at the strips with interest, so somehow I won't be surprised if next year all the houses start decorating their kirizome tree the same way.

Speak of the devil. Looks like Santa is here for us. It's pretty dark out, so the party will be starting soon.

"Hey, Yuki! Time to go to Seiichi's place!"

Yoki is yelling for me. Sure, sure. Guy's always in a hurry. It makes Miho mad: "I need to get ready before I can leave the house!" I'll bet right now he's in the entryway with Granny Shige on his back, waiting impatiently for me.

I just looked out the window. Santa was patting Noko on the head, and when he saw me he waved. I waved back.

Probably at tonight's party, Team Nakamura will raise some kind of ruckus. But I'm going to end the record here. I'm hungry, and Yoki is yelling, "Hurry it up!" and before you know it, it'll be spring again and time to concentrate on work in the mountains.

I think I'll probably stay on in Kamusari. I still don't know if I'm suited for this work or not. It's hard to say what kind of future I could have in a village with so few young people. I wonder if Nao and I could get married. Way too soon to be thinking about that, I know. And when I do start thinking about marriage, I miss Yokohama, where there are so many girls to choose from.

Still and all, there's a lot more I want to know about this village, the people living here, and the mountains.

One thing I do know: Kamusari village will go on forever, just as it always has. The people will go on with their easygoing ways, surrounded every day by the mountains and the river and the trees. Like the insects and birds and beasts and gods and every living thing in the village, the people, too, will go on being their ordinary, happy-go-lucky selves.

If you ever get in the mood, drop by. You're welcome anytime. Which is why I'm not showing this record to anyone. *Heh heh.*

Till next time!

ACKNOWLEDGMENTS

I received the help of a great many people in writing this book. I am deeply grateful to all those who spoke with passion about their experiences in the mountains and generously shared their knowledge and love of forestry and trees. Any deviation from fact in the novel, whether intentional or otherwise, is of course my own responsibility.

ORGANIZATIONS

Forestry Agency
Forestry Cooperative Owase
Kajimoto Fine Woods
Kumano Kodō Center
Kumano Kodō Owase
Mie Prefecture Bureau of Environment and Forests
Matsusaka Iinan Forestry Cooperative
Owase City Fishery, Agriculture and Forestry Division
Owase Cypress Interior Material Processing Cooperative
Owase Cypress Precut Cooperative
Owase Lumber Market
Takagi Lumber
Wood Make Kitamura

INDIVIDUALS

Chigusa Masanori

Fukunaka Mikio

Ichikawa Michinori

Ishihashi Naozō

Itō Masashi

Iwade Ikuo

Kajimoto Yoshitarō

Karasawa Michiko

Kitagawa Naoto

Kitamura Hidetaka

Kunita Masako

Kusu Hidetoshi

Matsunaga Miho

Mimbu Yasuyuki

Nagata Shin

Numata Masatoshi

Nomura Masami

Ogura Hiroshi

Okada Katsuyuki

Ōnishi Masayuki

Ozawa Makoto

Sada Issei

Shibata Eiichi

Sugimoto Miharu

Sudō Hiroshi

Takagi Toshio

Tobiyama Ryūichi

Wakabayashi Tetsuya

Yamaguchi Chikara

Yamaguchi Kazuaki

Yoshikawa Toshihiko

MAIN REFERENCES

Fifth Kikigaki Kōshien Executive Committee, ed. *Heisei 18 nendo daigokai mori no "kikigaki Kōshien" kikigaki sakuhinshū* (Verbatim accounts from the fifth forest "verbatim recording Kōshien" of 2006).

Forest Agency, ed. *Heisei 18 nendo shinrin ringyō hakusho* (2006 white paper on forests and forestry).

Niijima Toshiyuki. *Puro ga oshieru mori no waza, yama no sahō* (Lessons from a pro in forest skills and mountain etiquette). Zenkoku ringyō kairyō fukyū kyōkai, 2004.

Suzuki Isao. *Ha, mi, juhi de kakujitsuni wakaru jumoku zukan* (Picture encyclopedia of trees with clear identification by leaves, fruit, and bark). Nihon bungeisha, 2005.

Takada Hisao. Recorded verbatim by Shiono Yonematsu. *Yakushima no yamamori: Sennen no shigoto* (The mountain rangers of Yakushima: A thousand-year job). Soshisha, 2007.

ABOUT THE AUTHOR

Photo © Hiroyuki Matsukage

Shion Miura made her fiction debut in 2000 with *Kakuto suru mono ni maru* (*A Passing Grade for Those Who Fight*). In 2006, she won the Naoki Prize for her story collection *Mahoro ekimae Tada Benriken* (*The Handymen in Mahoro Town*). Her other novels include *Kaze ga tsuyoku fuiteiru* (*The Wind Blows Hard*), *Kogure-so monogatari* (*The Kogure Apartments*), and *Ano ie ni kurasu yonin no onna* (*The Four Women Living in That House*). *Fune o amu* (*The Great Passage*, translated by Juliet Winters Carpenter) received the Booksellers' Award in Japan in 2012 and an Earphones Award and was made into an award-winning motion picture. Miura has also published more than fifteen collections of essays and is a manga aficionado.

ABOUT THE TRANSLATOR

Photo © 2014 Toyota Horiguchi

Juliet Winters Carpenter is a professor emerita of Doshisha Women's College of Liberal Arts and a veteran translator. Her first translated novel, *Secret Rendezvous* by Kobo Abe, received the 1980 Japan-U.S. Friendship Commission Prize for the Translation of Japanese Literature. In 2014, her translation of *A True Novel* by Minae Mizumura received the same award, as well as the American Translators Association's Lewis Galantière Award. Besides Shion Miura's bestselling novel *The Great Passage*, her recent translations include *An I-Novel* by Minae Mizumura, *At the End of the Matinee* by Keiichiro Hirano, and *Pax Tokugawana: The Cultural Flowering of Japan, 1603–1853* by Tōru Haga. She and her husband live on Whidbey Island in Washington State.